Temperature Rising

BY

ALYSIA S. KNIGHT

Temperature Rising

By Alysia S. Knight
Published by Heart Dreams Press
Copyright © 2014 Alysia S. Knight
Cover design: by Kelli Ann Morgan @
www.inspirecreativeservices.com

ISBN:-1-942000-25-1
ISBN-13:978-1-942000-25-9

Also available from Alysia S. Knight

Լ☝౨౦

Past To Die For

Kare for Me

Blind Witness

Beauty and the Chief

Trail to Her Heart

His Governess

Her Brand of Trouble

The Ruins – Out of Time

My Spy

Where There's a Will

Aurora Rising

Whistleblower

Mindblower

The Olympus Game

Լ☝౨౦

To my family, I have been truly blessed.

I love you.

Chapter One

"Lady. Lady! Isn't this your stop?"

The bus driver gained Laken's attention enough for her to realize he was right. She stumbled her way off the bus. The rain felt blessedly cool against her skin. It had been the most awful day of her life.

With shaky fingers, she touched her forehead. It felt even hotter than earlier. A groan made it past her lips. She staggered slightly and wondered if anyone would notice if she sank to the sidewalk.

Her body trembled as chills raked her despite the fever. Her feet were the only place on her body that didn't seem to be burning up. They were freezing in what, that morning, had been her best leather pumps. The shoes were now water-soaked and ruined.

Forcing herself to put one foot in front of the other, Laken concentrated on the pharmacy sign halfway down the block. It became her beacon leading her through the dark, rainy night. Another hundred feet and she could get the flu medicine, then two blocks to her apartment and bed.

She could sleep late in the morning. Finally, after all the nights and weekends, the building plans were done, and the presentation wasn't until one. All she had to do now was make it home.

The cold glossy concrete beckoned her. Maybe she could just lie down and rest for a minute. She wavered on her feet. Her knees started to give out.

No, she forced herself to stiffen, focusing on the pharmacy sign. Fifty more feet. Laken concentrated on the doorway, counting each step she took. She made it to twenty then started again, unable to make her mind go any higher.

With her attention so locked on the doorway, she didn't even notice the woman until she cut her off. The woman's stride was quick and purposeful, full of energy, like Laken's normally was. They were close to the same age. Even their shoulder-length brown hair was similar, except the other woman's hair was still dry and springy due to the umbrella she carried. Laken had forgotten her umbrella that morning. One other major difference existed between them. The other woman looked alive and radiant. Laken knew she looked about at death's doorstep.

The woman disappeared into the drugstore. Laken forced herself to follow. Again, so intent on her destination, she didn't see the man until she collided with him in the doorway. The impact knocked what strength Laken had from her. She would've fallen if it weren't for the large hands that bit into her arms.

Laken caught the scent of sandalwood and musk over the stuffiness in her head. "Sorry." The words came out scratchy and hoarse from her throat. She raised her gaze up over the tall form covered in a black trench coat. The collar was turned up and a hat pulled low, hiding his face from her except the eyes.

The words of thanks died on her lips, cut off by pale, penetrating orbs which seared deep into her soul. The feverishness of his eyes didn't seem to be from a physical illness like hers, but there was something distinctively unhealthy about them. Laken found herself not wanting to speculate about what it was.

"Thank you." Laken managed to choke out, dropping her gaze.

Before she could pull back, his hand came up to touch

her face. He traced a finger along her sweaty brow, then he brought it to his lips.

"I know you now." The voice rumbled low and gravelly.

It tore at her like broken glass. He disappeared into the drugstore. A full minute passed before a shudder ran through her, breaking the spell. She managed to push her way into the store.

Thankfully, she didn't see the man. Laken looked down each aisle she came to, fearing he'd be there. Her anxiety ebbed at not seeing the man in the aisle she needed. The pharmacy window was closed, so she tried focusing on the different medicines. Her muddled mind took forever to make a decision.

Her relief grew when she didn't see the man at the checkout counter. The woman who entered before her stood there talking to the sales clerks.

"I'm celebrating," the woman boasted. "Those guys never knew what hit them. I pulled the promotion out from under them so smoothly I'm sure they're still scratching their balding, two-watt heads wondering what happened." As the woman laughed, one of the clerks broke away.

"Bad night?" the old man greeted Laken, stepping up to check her out.

"Yes." She managed to get out, fumbling for a twenty dollar bill.

"Not feeling good?"

"No." She took her change, not knowing or caring if it was correct.

"You better get home and take care of yourself."

"That's my plan." She pulled on her strength and managed an answer that sounded better than she felt. "Goodnight."

"Night," the man returned as she moved to the door.

Outside, the rain had stopped, but it didn't ease how Laken felt. In a stupor, she made it home, barely managing to swallow a dose of medicine and pull off her wet clothes before falling into bed.

The nightmare started immediately. Her heart pounded, ready to explode. The heat burned unbearable, a hunger of its own. She fought with the shadow, but it closed in, driving her farther into the darkness.

She tried to run, but foggy hands held her back. The ground itself clung to her legs. Fire consumed her. No matter how she struggled, she couldn't break free. The race was on. Death was at hand, she could feel it.

Long, powerful strides ate up the darkened alley. Exuberance rose in The Hunter. In front of Laken, a figure darted. She felt the fear in the woman, tasted the terror. It was so powerful. The Hunter's pace quickened, taking Laken with him, but still The Hunter didn't break into a run. Their prey was trapped. The Hunter could taste the victory. Fevered blood pumped hard. He savored the challenge, anticipated the kill. It sickened Laken.

Closer now, the prey stumbled and fell. She looked back over her shoulder, and for a moment, Laken looked into her own face, then it wasn't hers. It shifted, changed slightly, familiar but unknown. The fear which shadowed the woman's features spread into terror.

"No!" Laken saw the woman scream out as she reached for her. It wasn't her hand though. The hand which caught the woman had large, long fingers, undoubtedly masculine, encased in a black glove. Laken looked past the hand, back to the woman who was frozen in fear. Laken felt terror radiate up through the hand. The Hunter fed on it. A sense of power burst in him.

"Fight!" Laken tried to scream at her.

The command became lost in the excitement and adrenaline of The Hunter as he pulled the woman from the ground. Laken attempted to turn away, but was trapped as much as the woman. She fought to pull herself from the awful nightmare.

Finally, as if her struggling somehow seeped into the woman, she began to fight. The Hunter pulled her to him, wrapping an arm around her, holding her trapped against his body. Euphoria pounded through him. He looked down into the woman's eyes as he plunged the knife into her back.

Laken screamed for the woman as she watched her dropped, lifeless to the filth of the alley.

Satisfaction coursed through The Hunter as he leaned down and, with a couple careless swipes, wiped the knife off on the woman's sweater. He straightened, deliberately placed his foot on her back and ground it down before stepping over her. Task finished, he simply left, without so much as a glance back, finally, letting Laken slip free into oblivion.

CӠꝹ

"You're not going to like this."

"What do we have, Jonesy?" Spencer 'Mac' MacDaniels asked as he eased his six-foot-four body from the car. He towered seven inches over his partner, and that was just the beginning of the differences. Marcus Jones had a stocky, compact body like a bull and dark brown hair, while Mac had a lean waist, broad shoulders and sandy hair.

"Female, Caucasian, brown hair, age twenty-seven," Jonesy recited as he led the way down the alley. "Name's Andrea Chambers. They found her purse back there – intact. It had about eighty bucks in cash and her cards still in it, so definitely not a robbery."

"Is the team here?"

"Yeah, it's all being handled by the book. If there's anything, they'll find it."

Mac nodded, grimacing slightly as he stepped over a piece of trash and came down too hard on his left leg.

"You okay?" Jonesy asked.

After being partners for nearly three years, Mac

figured Jonesy knew what the answer would be. "Yeah." The leg that had taken a bullet three months earlier would never be the same again. Mac wondered just how long he had until he was forced into retirement.

Retirement − a couple months ago he couldn't have imagine such a thing. Then in a flash, a bust went wrong when a civilian stepped in the way. He'd been able to draw the fire away from the man who picked the wrong place and time to step out for a smoke. They got the shooter, but not before he got hit in the leg.

Mac wanted to shake his head at the stupidity of it. He was a good cop, a good detective. Some might even say great. He and Jonesy had the best record in the city. That's why he was back on duty, but for how long?

His thoughts shifted direction at the sight of the body lying amongst the trash, in a puddle of blood and water. He stayed back letting the crime scene guys do their work but took in the surroundings, cataloging each thing. They'd give him photos of every inch of the area. Still, he liked to get the layout firmly set in his mind. Gradually, he moved in as close as he dared, getting his first real look at the woman. She lay face down so there wasn't much he could tell.

"What've we got, Rob?" he asked the man doing the grid beside her.

The man looked back over his shoulder. "Hey, MacDaniels." The cheerfulness in the voice belied his profession. "How's it goin'?"

"A lot better for me than her. What can you tell me?"

"One stab wound to the back. Judging from the body and weather conditions, probably sometime last night. Give you a closer time later. I'd say she was facing the killer when she was stabbed. We'll have to get the Medical Examiner's report at the lab to confirm that and any other details. I do have one odd thing for you, though."

"What's that?" Jonesy said from beside him.

"See here." Rob pointed a gloved finger toward an area on the woman's back where there was a distinctive smudge spot.

"I'm getting a strong feeling that didn't happen when she fell." Jonesy studied the area.

"Nope. Whoever killed her stepped on her and not by accident. I'd say he deliberately smashed his foot down," the tech put forth.

"Like he was grinding her under his foot," Mac speculated so just his partner and the tech could hear.

"That's what it looks like to me," Rob agreed in a hushed tone.

"Do me a favor." Mac shifted his gaze away from the mark to the man. "Keep quiet about this, but give me extra pictures with measurements."

"Knew you were going to say something like that. I'm way ahead of ya. I'll pull anything I can from it."

"Thanks." Mac didn't doubt Rob. He liked working with the man. Rob was the best at what he did. They all fell silent. While Rob worked, Mac and his partner studied the scene, so they could discuss it later. It was one of the things that made them so good together. They both could take in a scene and then pull it back up, rehashing it until they dissected every detail.

Mac didn't like what he was getting. This was no accidental killing or domestic dispute. It had been planned, played out and executed. He could feel it and knew it would happen again.

og☙

Laken groaned and forced her eyes open. She wasn't dead, but she still felt awful. At least she wasn't burning up. With another groan, she pushed herself up from the damp sheets. Looking at the clock, it read eleven fifty-five. A wave of panic swept over her. She only had an hour to make it to the office.

Springing from the bed, she swayed, catching herself

on her dresser. She felt totally drained. However, she didn't think she was going to die anymore. A shiver of dread went through her as the vision of the nightmare flashed through her mind in horrifying clarity. Shaking it off, she stumbled to the bathroom. After a five minute shower she felt more refreshed.

Twenty minutes later, she hurried from the apartment. Luckily, the buses were with her, and she made it to the office in record time, getting off the elevator with ten minutes to spare.

"Laken, what are you doing here?" Kathy Martin, the architectural group secretary, exclaimed in way of greeting. "You're supposed to be home sick."

"We have the Sherman presentation. Don't worry, I'm already for it. As soon as it's over, I'm going back home to bed. I just couldn't miss this. I know they'll love my designs. I added some extra features that make them perfect." She let her enthusiasm boost her energy, but it faded quickly at the expression on the secretary's face.

"But, the presentation just ended. Mr. Hoster and Mr. Warner just took them to lunch." Kathy sounded consoling.

Laken felt a different kind of sickness wash over her and shook her head in denial. "It can't be. It has to be someone different. This is the Galaxy building, Mr. Sherman's presentation. It's not until one o'clock." Her stomach clinched as Kathy shook her head.

"It was at eleven." The woman tried to make it come out gently, but there was no softening the impact.

"But, when did they change it? Why didn't someone call me?"

"It wasn't changed. That's when it's always been scheduled for."

"But, Mr. Hoster said one." Laken dropped on the corner of the desk as her legs could no longer hold her up. "I was to get to present my plans. They were one of the top three." She raised a trembling hand to her forehead. "I

spent so much time on them. They were perfect. I know they would've been chosen." Her heart began to pound. "I can't believe, after all that work, they didn't let me present." Laken rubbed at her temple, trying to clear her thoughts. "He left me out on purpose. Why?"

"Now Laken, I can't believe that. Maybe it was because you were so sick. Still, after all that work, it doesn't seem fair. Listen, you'd better go home and get some more sleep. I'll mark that you were in today, so you can get a half day."

"Oh, what? Okay." Drained, Laken stood and swayed. As with the presentation, all strength had been ripped from her.

"Are you all right?" Kathy rose, coming around the desk to reach for her.

"Yeah." Laken steadied herself. "I just need to get home to bed."

"Can I get someone to drive you?"

"I can catch a cab." Laken swayed again.

"No, I'll get Eric to drive you. He has some deliveries to do anyway. You don't look so good."

CS&OD

Eight hours later, Mac placed his elbows on his desk and rested his head against them. He was tired. He had a headache and his leg throbbed. Maybe getting out of police work wasn't such a bad idea. Maybe he could meet a nice woman who wasn't dead. Someone he could go home to. That he could love. Maybe even have a family.

Oh, he knew a lot of guys on the force who had good marriages. His partner was one of them. Jonesy had a great marriage. But, Mac felt his own life was too full of the dark side. He'd gone right from rookie to narcotics for five years, most of it undercover. The last seven years he'd been in homicide, picking up the pieces of destroyed lives.

Neither had been conducive to meeting a nice woman. Both were hard on relationships. He knew — he'd tried.

With a sigh, he sat back, pulled open his drawer and got out the bottle of ibuprofen he kept there.

He hoped that would do the job on his head and leg. He almost wished for something stronger, but after working narcotics, he couldn't bring himself to take the pain pills the doctor had prescribed for him after leaving the hospital.

What he needed was sleep. Hopefully, there'd be some more information in the morning. It was time to follow Jonesy's example and go home. And, again, he thought it would be a whole lot sweeter if someone was there waiting.

CROD

The next morning, Laken felt much better as she hurried from the bus stop. She knew she probably should have stayed home again today, then she'd have a long weekend to get better, but she couldn't wait until Monday to talk to Mr. Hoster. She wanted an explanation why he'd given her the wrong time. She'd gone over it again and again in her mind and knew it hadn't been an accident. No doubt about it, but, she didn't understand why. He had always seemed respectful, and appreciated her work.

Anger surged through her again. He knew how hard she'd worked on the plans. Why would he cut her out of the meeting? What could've been the purpose of not letting her present? She wished she could blame it on being sick, but inside, she knew that wasn't the reason. The proof was in all their interaction for the week. He'd always stressed the one o'clock time. After all that work, he'd done it on purpose.

The tears that had plagued her since the day before well up. She was not going to cry, she told herself. Pushing back the hurt, clinging to the pain, she let her anger build. She would get an explanation. Her plans had been good. They were more than good. They were amazing, and they would have been chosen. She could ring Hoster's neck.

For months now, she'd been wondering about her position at the company. Waiting for the opportunity to move up, or wondering if she should just move on. Living in the big city didn't fit her, especially not the single life there. Hanging out at bars and talking with strangers was not her forte. And, though she worked in a male dominated office, it didn't take her long to understand inter-office dating was not a good idea.

About eight months earlier, her social life had fallen to non-existent. Which left a lot of time in the evenings to work on plans, but she wanted a social life. She wanted to find someone special. To be honest, she wanted that more than she wanted her designs to be picked. Why couldn't she have both? Well, she might not be able to do much about her love life, but she could find out why Hoster excluded her and what her future held at the Warner Agency. She turned down the hall.

"You look better today," Kathy greeted as she approached.

"I feel better, just a little draggy."

"Maybe you should've taken another day," Kathy suggested.

"I'm fine. I'll have the weekend to really rest up. Is Hoster in?" Laken glanced at the closed office door.

"Yes, but he left a do not disturb for the next couple hours."

A wave of frustration rolled over Laken. She wanted answers − now. Resigned, she looked back at Kathy. "Will you setup an appointment for me before lunch?"

"Sure, eleven-thirty good?"

"Yes."

Laken didn't think eleven thirty would ever get there. The morning dragged on forever. At twenty after, she left her drafting table and went to the ladies room to freshen up and steel herself for the confrontation. At twenty-five after, she strode up Kathy's desk.

"I'm so sorry, Laken, I just tried to call you. Mr. Hoster hurried out a couple minutes ago. He said he had an important meeting and wouldn't be back until Monday." Kathy sounded genuinely upset. "I tried to tell him you wanted to talk to him."

Laken's stomach churned. The snake! She had no doubt that he had avoided her on purpose. Her heart pounded with frustration. "Can you set me an appointment for first thing Monday morning?" She ground the words out.

"I'll make it nine-fifteen. He's usually here by then," Kathy answered.

Of course, Laken thought, not like her eight o'clock or earlier. "Thanks," she forced out a weak smile. The smile faltered as she noticed the newspaper lying on the corner of Kathy's desk.

Fear waved over her. In a flash, Laken saw the terror-filled face looking up at her as the black-gloved hand reached down. Laken staggered. Lights slashed through her mind. Buzzing rang in her ears. For a minute, she thought she would faint. Kathy must have thought so too because the next thing Laken knew, Kathy had her by the elbow, easing her down on the chair by her desk.

"You should never have come in today," the woman was saying.

"No, I'm okay. Sorry." Laken drew in a deep breath and reached for the newspaper. "The woman." She couldn't get any more out, starring down at a picture of the woman in her nightmare.

"Oh, that. Mr. Hoster dropped the paper on my desk as he left. I was just reading it. Scary." Kathy looked over to her in concern. "Did you know her?"

"I think I've seen her before."

"She worked in the building across the quad. And, actually, she wouldn't have lived far from you. She was killed only a couple blocks from her apartment."

The word 'killed' hit Laken like a blow of icy wind, chilling her to the bone. "How was she killed?" She knew with a sick dread what the answer was going to be.

"Stabbed. Listen, I think you'd better head back home. You look really pale again."

"I'm fine. Do you mind if I look at the paper for a minute?"

"No, go ahead." The secretary handed it to her, with a watchful eye.

The article didn't say much more than Kathy had already told her. Except the body was found in an alley not far from where Laken lived, and the police were looking for anyone who had information about the attack. Images poured through her mind in vivid detail, the chase, the fear, the exultation of The Hunter. Laken's heart pounded bringing with it a wave of nausea.

"Laken, are you all right?" The words finally got through to her.

"Yes, but I think I'm going to take your advice and leave now."

"Good. Get some rest and don't come in Monday if you don't feel all better."

"I'll be fine, and I'll be here for that appointment." The only way she was going to miss it was if she were dead. A shiver went through her, and she took one last glance at the newspaper.

Laken really did plan to go home when she gathered her purse and jacket, but when the bus stopped in front of her instead of getting on she turned away and started walking. Her mind locked in a vision of murder as it played over and over again in her mind. She had no conscious thought of where she was going or what she was going to do until, over an hour later, she found herself standing in front of the old, gray brick building of the police station.

"No, no way," she said to herself as she placed a foot on the first step. She couldn't walk in there and say she saw a murder in her dream. They'd think she was a wacko who got kicks harassing police, or plain psycho and she'd find herself locked up in a mental ward.

She tried to make herself turn as she took the next step, then the image of the woman in the paper came to her mind and she took the last three. At the door, she paused again and almost won the battle to turn away, when a man came out and held the door for her.

Laken swallowed hard and stepped inside. She felt sick again. She shouldn't be here. Heat waved over her. She should be home in bed, instead of being ushered through a metal detector.

Laken stared around the large lobby, not sure where to go or what to do. To the side of the door was a large staircase, next to it a set of elevators. Chairs filled with people were lined in two rows, backs together, in the center of the room. Directly ahead a tall, hardwood counter took up a good portion of the wall, several uniformed officers stood behind it.

"May I help you?" one officer said directly to her.

She managed to pull her resolve around her and step forward. "I think so." She forced a swallow as her voice shook. "I'd like to speak with someone about the murder."

"Which murder?" the man asked off-handedly.

How many murders did they get? Laken almost asked, and then decided she really didn't want to know. "The one in the paper, the woman who was stabbed in the alley." Funny, she couldn't think of the name but would never forget the face.

Chapter Two

"I was thinking last night. It might not be too bad having to get out of police work." Mac decided it was time to run the idea by his partner.

Jonesy hardly missed a beat before answering. "But that's what you're good at."

"Yeah." He turned the car into his parking place at the station. "But I want more out of life." He waited until they were both out of the car before he continued. "I'd like to find someone, get married and maybe have a family."

"So you're feeling your clock ticking? I thought that was a woman thing."

Mac sent him a scowl. "Funny."

Jonesy laughed then seemed to shrug it off. "Look, its natural. Your mortality's kicking in. You got shot and could've died."

"When did you become a shrink?"

"On-the-job training."

Mac couldn't argue that.

"Listen; give it some time before you make any drastic changes."

"It's not just that. It's …" Mac paused. "I'm not going to pass the physical."

"You don't know that."

Mac stopped and Jonesy turned to face him. "Yes, I do and I'm not going to be responsible for making Connie a widow." Jonesy was about to say something but Mac stopped him raising his hand. "I'm putting your life in danger every time we go out on a call."

"I rather have you at my back than anybody."

"Yeah, well." He started walking again. "It's more than that. It's wanting a woman to look at me like I'm special to her. Coming home to someone, going to bed and sliding my arms around a woman and knowing she's mine. Feeling love and being loved."

"Regular sex isn't bad either," Marcus Jones added with a grin.

"I can only imagine." Mac shifted his stride to take the stairs with his good leg leading.

"There's nothing stopping you."

"I'm not the casual sex kind of guy and way past the bar scene thing. Doing what I do doesn't really give me many possibilities. And by the time I get home, I'm burned out anyway. You're one of the lucky ones. Look around you." He pushed through the station doors. "These are the people I meet every day."

People crowded the room, most looked upset. Both men knew they were probably there to file a complaint. "And these are the live ones that I'm not trying to throw into a cell. How am I supposed to find a nice woman here?"

"How about that woman over there?" Jonesy laughed and pointed to a gray-haired woman that Mac figured stood all of five feet – if she could straighten her hunched shoulders. "She looks nice."

"Oh yeah, thanks, and if I was twice my age it might be decent."

Jonesy laughed again. "I bet she makes great cookies, though."

Mac didn't try to hold back another scowl as he pushed the elevator button. "Thanks a lot."

"Come on. There are women around. What about that nurse? She liked you."

"And had two other boyfriends she was juggling. No thanks."

"Okay, what about the physical therapist? She seemed pretty decent and interested."

"Until she found out I was a cop."

"Has a thing about cops?"

"Oh yeah, had to work on too many of them. Doesn't want anything personal to do with us, too high risk," Mac stressed.

"You know Connie could set you up."

"Nah, no way. That's asking for trouble. I like your wife too much to get on her bad side. If I dated one of her friends, and it didn't work out, what would ..." His voice petered out as he saw the woman at the desk talking to Hammond.

"Hey, MacDaniels, this one's for you." It wasn't until his mind answered, *she sure is*, that he realized Hammond had really called to him. When the woman turned toward him, he almost repeated the words out loud.

It only took a second for him to make an assessment – pretty, nice, lost. She looked totally out of place. There was an uncertain anxiety about her. If he didn't miss his guess, she wanted to get out of there.

Her eyes darted to the door, and Mac knew he was about to lose her. He moved into her path. The green eyes shifted right to him, and even from ten feet away, he could see the gold flecks in them. They were incredible eyes. There was no toughness about them, which meant she was a victim. That kicked up the protective instinct in him, and he headed for her ready to slay dragons.

Behind him he could hear Jonesy still talking. "You know Connie wouldn't do that. Mac ... Mac?"

The woman turned back toward Hammond. Several people moved in Mac's path, but he kept a lock on the woman.

Jonesy moved beside him. "See something interesting?"

"I think so."

Mac studied her as he approached. Her height would've been about five-eight, and though she wore boots with about three inch heels, she was still perfect for him. She had on a brown sweater that hugged her curves and a swirly patterned skirt that flared at the top of the boots. Her light-brown hair hung long and straight around her shoulders. He'd interviewed enough women to know the look was called dressy casual. For him, it was just appealing.

Her hands swung out as she talked, and his vision locked on the left one. No ring, he acknowledged with a surge of pleasure. Then her voice reached him, velvet soft, though it was laced with hesitancy. "I shouldn't have bothered you. It isn't important. I'm sorry." She turned and stepped right into him. "Oh," she gasped out.

He caught her under her elbows and steadied her. Her green eyes came up to his face and stayed there. Obviously shocked, but he wondered if something else held her like it did him.

Oh, yes, she was for him. The thought came once more. "You wanted me?" He got the words out.

"I …" She swayed slightly, and he steadied her again.

"Mac, she needed to talk to someone about the Chambers murder," the sergeant at the desk spoke up behind her.

That got his attention. It shouldn't have surprised him though, because if she needed to talk to him, it had to involve a murder.

"Won't you come with me?" He kept a hold of one elbow, stepping to the side to direct her to the elevator.

"I'm sorry. I shouldn't have bothered you." She stumbled over the words.

He knew she was going to flee if he didn't act fast. "No bother. I'm Detective Spencer MacDaniels. This is my partner, Marcus Jones."

Like a good partner, Jonesy maneuvered to the other

side of her, effectively trapping her in between them. Luckier still, the elevator opened, and they were able to usher her in before she could turn away.

"Laken Williams," she returned hesitantly. He figured she answered more out of manners than really wanting to say.

"Laken." He let her name slide over him. "I like it. It's different. I don't think I've ever met anyone named Laken before."

"It's not very common." She glanced furtively over at him. "I really think it best I leave before I waste your time."

"Why don't you let me decide? First, let's get settled at my desk and you can tell me what brought you here."

Her eyes went from him to Jonesy and back again.

Mac could tell she wanted to decline but her shoulders slumped in resignation.

"I have a call to follow up on," Jonesy announced as they approached their desks. "I'll catch up to you in a minute."

Mac sent his partner a look of thanks. Once they were settled, he turned to her. "Now, how can I help you? Were you a friend of Miss Chambers?" He felt a wave of relief when she shook her head. So he wasn't dealing with someone torn up because of the loss of a friend, but she was – unsettled. That fit her he decided.

"Then," he started gently, "you have some information for me."

"I don't know." The words burst from her. "This is all a mistake. I'm not sure what I was thinking. Well, I was thinking maybe I could help, but I can't. I'm sorry. I really need to go."

Mac reached over the corner of the desk and caught her hand. It was soft. She had long fine fingers. He rubbed his thumb over her knuckles, and she seemed to ease. "Let's start with the basics, name."

"Laken Ann Williams." It came out shaky, but she

gave it to him and started to relax.

Across the room someone slammed a file drawer and swore. She jerked and the nervousness flooded right back in.

"I'm not some nut case," she blurted out.

He couldn't keep back a smile. "That's nice to know. What are you?"

"An architect. I really am quite logical. I'm not sure how to explain this. But, I'm not lying or making it up."

"It's okay. Why don't you tell me your address and phone number?" he urged softly.

"All right, I just want you to understand." She steadied herself in the chair, and he saw the strength under the nervousness.

A lot of people were nervous around police, like they were afraid they were going to be arrested for just being around them. He'd have to get her to see him as just a man.

His attention caught on her address. It was less than three blocks from where they found the victim. "Good, now why don't you tell me what you know?"

Again it was plain to read her hesitation and how she worked formulating what she wanted to give him. He felt a kick of sadness that she wouldn't just open up.

She locked her fingers together in her lap. "I think I saw the killer."

Her words took him by surprise. He expected her to wash over things or lie. He leaned forward, feeling his excitement rise over his interest in her as a woman, and she became a witness. "You saw the killer?"

"I think ..." she hesitated, "... I did."

Laken wasn't sure what to say. She should never have come here but she had to do something. She couldn't let him kill again, and she knew he would. He was a predator – a hunter. She remembered that clearly.

"Can you give me a description?"

She jerked at the question and looked at the detective

and felt a touch of longing. This would be easier if she didn't feel so many emotional shifts since meeting him. She didn't know what it was about him, but he disturbed her already unbalanced senses. She needed all her wits about her if she was going to come out of this without sounding like a fruitcake, and she was having trouble getting past how her heart jumped every time she looked at him.

She took a deep breath. Okay, she could do this. Then he'd think she was nuts, and she would never see him again, but she had tried to do what was right. Still, she felt a sense of loss and pushed past it. "Not really, I couldn't see much of him. He had a raincoat on and a hat with a wide brim. It was pulled down low on his face. He wasn't as tall as you, six foot – maybe six-one."

"And how tall do you think I am?"

I'd say close to six-three."

"Good, I'd like you to tell me everything. Where you saw the man, what you saw leading up to that time and what you witnessed?"

She took a deep breath. "Two nights ago, Wednesday, I was coming home late from work. I took the bus to Wilken. I'm not sure what time exactly, after eight thirty but before nine. I wasn't feeling good. I had a fever. All I could think of was getting to the pharmacy and getting some medicine. Just before I got there, I noticed a woman." The tremor shook her voice. "She was the one from the picture in the newspaper. She went into the pharmacy before me."

"Did you recognize her? Had you seen her before?"

"No. I don't think so."

"Can you tell me what she was wearing?"

Laken thought for a moment, suppressing the image of the attack as it tried to surface. "A tan raincoat, nylons so she was wearing a skirt or dress."

She waited while he made a couple notes.

"Continue, please."

"I really wasn't paying much attention around me. I was concentrating on getting through the door. That's why I didn't see him. I don't know if he was watching her or not, but we ran into each other. Actually, it was probably me who ran into him. I don't know. When we hit, he caught hold of me to keep me from falling." Her throat tightened. "I … it … he frightened me."

"Miss Williams. Miss Williams. Laken," he prompted her, bringing her attention back to him.

"Yes, sorry."

"What frightened you?"

"The cold hatred I felt."

"You felt?" he urged softly.

"Yes, when he touched my brow." She shivered, slipping back to the moment.

"He touched you?"

"Yes, he wiped his finger across my brow then licked it."

"He licked your brow." His glaze flickered to the side, and she noticed that Jonesy had come up.

She shook her head as she looked back to Detective MacDaniels. "No, his finger."

"Did he do anything else?"

Her heart thundered. "He said he had my taste now."

The detectives exchanged looks.

"Did he say anything else?" Detective Jones spoke up.

"No, he went into the store."

"You think the other woman was our victim?" Jones asked again.

"It was her," she said firmly.

"All right," MacDaniels tried to calm her. "Describe him."

"I can't, other then what I already gave you."

"You looked right at him. He touched you, and you can't describe him."

She jerked at Jones's remarks.

"It was dark and rainy. He had a large, black raincoat on. The collar was up, the hat pulled down. It was wide brimmed, kind of like the Indiana Jones type. All I could really see of his face were his eyes. They were pale, that's all I could tell." She felt panic rise in her voice but couldn't stop it.

"It's all right," MacDaniels soothed. "What happened next?"

"Nothing. I went home, took some medicine and went to bed. I didn't know about the murder until I saw her picture in the paper."

Mac felt his stomach clench. She was holding something back, he knew it. But what and why, after she had come down here. She really wanted to help. He sensed that.

"What makes you think it was him?" Jonesy's question scored a hit by the way she jerked.

"Because, I know." The stress level was high in her voice. She sounded desperate.

Mac hated to but knew he had to add to the pressure. He went in with a different tactic. "I understand he frightened you, Miss Williams, but that is no reason to believe he killed her."

"But, he did it."

"What else did you see, Laken?" he pressed.

"Nothing."

"Then why do you sound so certain?" He shot the question at her, keeping his tone sharp.

"Because I am."

"There is no way. We couldn't even arrest him on what you gave us." His voice went cold, flat.

"I gave you all I can."

The pleading in her eyes cut into him. He felt it like he had never felt anything before. "No, you didn't," Mac countered. "What aren't you telling us? What did you see?"

"Nothing."

"Then you couldn't know it was him." He leaned forward, bearing down on her.

"Yes, I do," she cried out and the flood gates opened. "He hunted her down, and when he caught her, he pulled her up, and looked down into her eyes and stabbed her in the back. Then he just let her drop to the ground and stepped on her."

He knew it. The exaltation coursed through him. He had a witness. The satisfaction faded by the look on her face as she realized what she'd said. Her face dropped into her hands. He reached for her. His hand hovered over her, not sure what to do. "Laken, I need you to tell me everything you saw."

Her shoulders dropped in defeat and her body shook. "I didn't see it."

"Miss Williams, don't lie," he pressed. "You said he stabbed her in the back. And he stepped on her. We didn't release that information, and only about a dozen people associated with the case know it." He let it hang there.

Jonesy picked up the line. "Miss Williams, it's illegal to withhold information besides the fact that this person could kill again."

There was a sharp intake of breath. "He will kill again. I could feel it," she murmured, raising her head, pleading filled her eyes. "I want to help. That's why I'm here."

"Then why won't you help us?" Mac asked.

"I'm trying to, you just don't understand." Her shoulder's dropped again. "I don't understand."

"You're right. I don't understand, so why won't you tell me?" Mac softened his voice.

She shook her head in defeat.

"You can back up to the pharmacy and go over it again. That was all correct?" he prodded.

"Yes," she whispered.

"The description?" he questioned.

"That's all there is. Everything I remember."

"All right, after you left. What then?"

"I went home to bed just like I said. I'd been overworking. I was very sick. I was burning up."

"Then how did you know she was stabbed in the back while facing him, and how can you say he'll kill again?"

"Because I saw it in a dream." Her outcry did nothing to soften the blow of her words.

Mac figured the same doubt that shadowed Jonesy's face settled over his. The woman looked like she wanted to crawl into a hole.

"You're saying you're psychic?" Detective Jones's voice was laced with skepticism.

"No!" Laken denied, looking from one to the other. "No. Nothing like this has ever happened to me before. I keep hoping I'm wrong but I know I'm not. I saw the look of fear on her face the moment before he thrust the knife in her. I felt his thrill of invincibility as he took her life. There was no remorse, only pleasure, deep gratifying pleasure. He killed her, and he will kill again."

Mac felt his thrill of having a witness slipping away, but there was another sense of loss that went far deeper. For the first time in a long time, he'd felt a rush of interest, and the woman was mental. He wanted to honestly give her the benefit of the doubt and concede the possibility. But unfortunately, the only exposure he had was with psychics who were total frauds, people wanting fame, to feel important or different, and then some just preying on others' pain.

He ached with the disappointment that this woman would fit into one of those categories. Shoving his exasperation down, he rocked back in his chair, shoving his fingers through his hair, trying to regain his composure.

"You're saying you dreamed it?" He fought to keep his words even.

"Yes." There was a definite tremble in the answer.

"You were home sick?" By the pallor of her face, he

could believe that.

"Yes."

"And, you saw him kill her in your dream?"

Yes."

"But, you can't tell us what he looked like, other than the description of the man you ran into on your way home?"

"Yes." Again, it was the one-word answer.

They were supposed to be courteous to everyone, even crackpots, but Mac wanted to yell at her so bad he had to hold his breath to keep it in. In the middle of his reflections, Jonesy picked up the questioning, moving around the desk beside him.

"If you could see her clearly enough to recognize her from one brief sighting, while you were sick, to know it was her in the paper, then why can't you give us a better description of him?" Jonesy asked.

Great question, Mac thought, that should get her. Her answer froze him.

"Because, I saw it from his angle." Her choked words were enough to shock him. "Look, I'm sorry, I wasted you're time. I can't help you." She stood quickly. "It was a mistake to come here." She turned, heading for the stairs, and though she never broke into a run, she disappeared before they had time to decide to go after her, not that either tried.

"Man." Jonesy finally broke the silence. "I thought we had a real witness there for a minute."

"Me, too." Mac had to agree, but he'd felt he had something more ripped away. Laken Williams had touched him deeply.

"I've had enough of this." Marcus let out a sigh. "I've put in nine hours today already. I promised Connie a movie tonight. I say we call it a day and let the other team worry about it for a while."

"What?" Mac had to force his attention back to his

partner. "Oh, yeah, deal." He looked at the paper he'd been writing information on. Mac let out a sigh of his own, he placed it in his drawer and closed it with bitter finality.

Chapter Three

Laken didn't slow down in her rush to leave the building until she reached the park across the street. She wanted to be away from the men, from their questions and their doubts. She wanted to be home, only she just couldn't make it. Drained and shaky, she sank down on the grass under a tree and dropped her head wearily into her hands.

Frustration flowed through her. She'd only been trying to help, but their questions had made her feel guilty. Maybe she was for not finding some way to stop the psycho, which was foolishness. She hadn't actually been there. She hadn't even believed it was real until she saw the picture in the paper.

How was she supposed to stop him? The thought hit her hard, and she shook her head. She was an architect with her own problems at the moment. What did she know about catching killers? A big fat nothing.

She collapsed back against the tree. It wasn't her responsibility, but he was going to kill again. She would never forget what she saw – what she felt.

Someway, she needed to stop him if she wanted to save her own sanity, but how? She came back to that simple question again. The police didn't believe her. The pang she felt in her heart ripped deep, like a great sense of loss she didn't understand. Maybe she was going insane.

With a groan, she tried to keep herself from throwing up. The hate and anger of The Hunter still burned in her. She didn't want to remember it, but it was like it had infested her. She had to find a way to stop him, or she was afraid it would never leave. But for now what she needed to rest. Maybe get some sleep, but she was afraid to close her eyes, afraid of what she might see.

C3&O

Mac didn't know what drew his eyes across the street to the park, but he could hardly believe what he saw. There she was, sitting on the ground as if she'd just dropped there. Her head was bent to the ground. She looked defeated, and he hated the thought that he had helped do that to her.

It was sheer luck that he didn't send up a chorus of horns as he cut across the street, not paying attention to cars. He kept his gaze locked on the woman.

"Miss Williams." He wasn't sure what else to say. "Are you all right?"

A tiny mirthless laugh came from her, and she tilted her head up. "Don't worry, detective, I'm not going to go all psycho on you."

The beautiful green and gold eyes were red rimmed, but he couldn't tell if she'd been crying. He started to squat down in front of her, but when his leg protested with a jab of pain, he settled on the grass beside her instead. "I wasn't worried about you going psycho. I was wondering if you were all right."

"Let's see, I've been sick, had nightmares of someone being murdered, had the worst two days ever with my career, made a fool of myself to the police so they think I'm a nut case, if not possibly a killer. I'm not sure if I am all right."

Mac wasn't sure how to come back to that. Before he could formulate a comment, she started to talk again.

"I'm sorry. Sarcasm doesn't become me. I don't know why I said that, besides that it really has been a bad day."

"What happened?" He studied her.

"You really want to know?"

31

"Yes, I do. I'm interested."

She hesitated only a moment before she began. "I told you I'm an architect. Two months ago the president at the firm I work for announced the opportunity for anyone in the firm to work up a design for a big new project. We were given the guidelines and specs to go by, it was open for rough drawings to be done in a week then the top three were to be picked.

"Mine was one of the top three. We were then given two months to do the complete plans. Unfortunately, I still had to do my other assigned work. So, all of my free time for the last two months has been spent working on the plans: nights, weekends, all of it. But I got my plans done, and they were good. Honestly, very, very good if I do say so myself.

One problem though – I kind of wore myself out. That's how I got sick. Anyway, yesterday was to be the presentation at eleven o'clock. I was told it was at one by my supervisor. I'd been sick so came in late. The presentation was already done when I got there."

"Wait a minute, so after all that work, you didn't get to present your plans?" Mac homed right in on the bottom line.

"Actually, I did find out today that my plans were presented."

"Well, at least, that's good." He tried to sound positive.

"Yes, but the point is there was no change in the time. I was told one o'clock, more than once. And now my supervisor is avoiding me."

"You think he set it so you'd miss the appointment?"

"I know he did. I wasn't told the wrong time by mistake. I'm sure it was on purpose, but what I can't figure out is why. I've worked for the company since I graduated. Four years. I do good work, but this was my first big chance to show what I can do on my own."

"You really wanted this?"

"Yes, I've been wondering lately if I want to stay here in the city. I'm a small town girl. I don't fit in well with the crowds and the dating scene here. You can call me old fashioned. Actually, I've been called that and a few other things because I won't play the normal games, like believing I owe the guy a make-out session for taking me out. Anyway, if I get this contract, it would say I could make it. Either way, I'm thinking it's time to go off on my own, but I wanted to know I could make it first. It would have been a big feather in my cap."

Unconsciously, Mac shifted and started to massage a cramp out of his leg. "You're not the only one contemplating a career change."

"What happened?" She nodded to his leg.

"Big confrontation," he surprised himself when he started to tell her. He'd become good at brushing it off. But for some reason, he wanted her to know. "We about had this guy who had killed three people in a string of robberies. Then this civilian walked right into the bust. There were police all around, and he didn't even notice us."

"You got him out of the way." It was a statement not a question.

"Yeah, the gunman had turned on him. I was able to knock him away and draw the fire, but I got hit in the process. The jacket took the bullet that would've killed me. The blow is like getting hit with a sledge hammer. Knocked the breath out of me, and hurt so bad, it took me a minute before I realized I was hit in the leg." He shrugged his shoulders.

"You're quite a man." The words seemed to slip free as if she'd thought them but hadn't really meant to say them.

Heat spread through him at the look she gave him. "No different than the rest of the guys in that building." He tilted his head toward the station.

"As I said, you're quite a guy."

Mac felt himself growing hotter. "You aren't a cop groupie are you?"

She looked thoughtful. "I don't think I've ever really known a police officer before." She tilted her head to one side to look at him. "So, you're thinking of retiring?"

"I don't think I have much of a choice. I'm back on duty until the doctors decide how much of a recovery there will be, but I already know. I'm not going to pass the physical when it comes time. I can't run, can't jump. If I get more movement back, it will be passable, and with a brace when I play sports, I can have a decent active life. But, not as an officer, not when someone's life might depend on me."

"When will you know?"

"In a couple weeks."

"You sound like you've accepted it."

"I have. I don't have much choice. I think I was a good cop but its time. I had been feeling like I was ready for a change before. I've been too centered on the darkness in life. I worked narcotics right out of the academy, then homicide since. With either, you don't get to see the good. I'm ready for the good."

"You're not married?"

"No. I was kind of tied to the job when I got out of the academy, and as I say the dark side. I'm not saying my life is all bad. I've made some good friends along the way, and I have a good family. My parents and sister's family live a couple hours upstate. When I need a break, I head up to visit them." Mac couldn't believe he'd told her that.

"So what is your plan?"

"Believe it or not, I have a teaching degree. The three years of narcotics I spent undercover as a college student. I passed all my classes. I have a degree in teaching with a minor in forensic science. There's a university about halfway between here and my hometown that's looking for a professor. I have all the qualifications listed so I sent them a resume. I made it through the first interview to the short list. I'm still waiting to hear back. You know the old saying, 'those who can't do, teach'."

"No, I don't believe that about you," she said firmly. "You're more than that. You don't just survive, you come out on top."

Looking in her eyes, he could see she truly believed what she said. It felt amazing to have her look at him like that. Still, it was a bit embarrassing. "I don't have the job yet, and I don't know what kind of a teacher I will be."

"What kind do you think you'll be?"

He had to think about that. "A pretty good one. I've taught a couple classes at the academy that went well. I had a couple professors that I liked, and tried to emulate them."

"I think you'll be great."

"Oh really, and how's that?"

"I've gone from feeling pretty devastated to feeling comfortable around you in a matter of minutes. It says you have an honest way around people, and that counts for a lot."

"I'm sorry I hurt you."

"It's okay." She gave a self-derisive smile. "It's been one of those days. In fact, I really should get home and take care of myself, so I don't get sick again." She started to stand.

Mac used the tree for help as he followed the motion, and then caught her as she swayed on her feet. The action knocked him back against the tree. He braced his back against it and locked his arms around her, holding her to him. "Easy." He steadied her. "Are you okay?" Concern flooded him along with awareness of her body pressed against his.

Her head dropped to his chest. She took in a couple deep breaths before she pulled back. "Sorry, I was a little upset and missed lunch. I guess my blood sugar level's low. I'm okay now, thanks." She moved back, still slightly

ALYSIA S. KNIGHT

shaky.

"No problem." He missed the contact with her. "Are you going to be all right to drive?"

"I took the bus. I came from work, and for getting there – it's always easiest to take the bus and not pay for parking."

"All right, I'll give you a ride home then." A surge of pleasure jumped in him. "In fact, I have a better idea. Would you like to have dinner with me?"

"I think I'd better point out before saying anything else that you think I'm either a phony psychic or a nut case."

"Well, since I haven't decided yet, why don't we settle for I think you're fascinating and would like to spend some time with you?" He grinned, watching her face change to a look of amazement.

The laugh that escaped her seemed to catch her as much by surprise as it did him.

"I would really like to have dinner with you," he said, repeating the invitation.

Her eyes scanned his face a second before the answer slipped out. "Yes."

Elation soared through him as he held his hand out to her.

೫೦

Laken settled back in the chair, oddly content, enjoying the warmth of fire near their table. Dinner had been wonderful. She couldn't remember when she'd spent such an enjoyable evening. There was something about Detective MacDaniels – Mac – that she found very appealing. And it wasn't just his looks, though he looked real nice. She just hadn't felt this good on a date for a long time, if ever – not that it was really a date.

"This is a great restaurant." She looked around the quaint room with the brightly colored, carved chair and tiles that turned the hole-in-the-wall Mexican restaurant into a delightful place. "How did you find it?"

"Investigating a case."

"Someone was killed here." Laken felt an instant of distress until he calmed her.

"No, it was a former employee."

She relaxed back.

"You look like you're about to fall asleep there."

"I feel so much better. You were so right, that *Arroz-con-Pollo* was incredible, the perfect choice."

"I'm glad you liked it. I guess I should take you home."

He sounded reluctant.

"I've had a good time. I'm usually too nervous on dates to have plain fun. I guess having you already think I'm a fruitcake, I can't go any lower, so I might as well be myself."

"I've enjoyed being with you."

The heat in his eyes made her heart jump. A rush of warmth seeped into her cheeks. "Thank you."

She rose with him, making their way out. "I hate to have you take me home." She sighed.

The heat flared in his eyes as he looked back.

"Oh, sorry, I didn't mean that to sound like. I wasn't inviting you to− That is, I wasn't−"

"It's okay, Laken."

"I just don't want you to think I would hop into bed with you. It's not just you. Oh man, for a smooth evening, I just made a hash out of that." She paused, and glanced at him. He looked as if he was about to laugh at her. Then he did laugh out loud when she groaned and dropped her head in her hands.

She joined in the laugh when she looked up at him. "Maybe you better take me home now."

A few minutes later, they turned the next corner, and everything she was going to say fled her mind as her eyes locked on the pharmacy sign ahead.

"Laken, is something wrong?"

"I know you don't believe me." She turned to him. "But I'm going to ask you for a favor. Will you stop at the pharmacy up there? That's the one. Just ask if they remember seeing her that night, please," she added when he looked toward her.

Mac pulled into an open spot, put the car in park and turned to her. "I've been putting this off, but I have to ask. How did you know he stabbed her in the back and stepped on her?"

The remaining pleasure of the evening evaporated. "That was why you took me out, so you could finally interrogate me."

"No," he came back quickly. "I've been avoiding asking you, though I knew I had to. When you left the station, I figured I'd come find you tomorrow. I need to know how you know."

"Then I was right. It happened like I said."

"Laken."

"No, Mac. I didn't lie to you. It was all the truth, every bit of it, the guy here and the dream." She could see the doubt on his face, and it hurt down to the center of her heart. She turned away unable to take the look any longer. "Just go ask them."

"You really want me to believe you're psychic?"

"I'm not psychic." She wanted to scream but fought for composure. "I don't know how, but it was a dream. The worst dream I've ever had in my life. I was so sick I thought I was going to die."

"Maybe you were so sick, you really were there and don't remember it."

She could see him searching for explanations, and it just hurt more.

"No." She pushed open the door and headed for the pharmacy. She was halfway there before he caught her, but she refused to acknowledge him. She didn't see either of the people from two nights ago there when she entered the store. Going straight to the counter, she waited in silence until the woman behind the counter turned her attention to them.

"Good evening," Mac spoke up first as he took out his badge. "I'm Detective MacDaniels. I'd like to ask you a couple questions if I could?"

The woman looked at the badge and nodded.

"Were either of you here two nights ago?" He looked at both and received negative responses. "Could you please look up who was here and when they will be in again? I have a couple questions about a crime that happened not far from here that night and wanted to ask if they saw anything."

The woman went to a clipboard and wrote something then returned, handing him the paper. Mac glanced up and nodded. "Thank you."

Laken headed for the door, not waiting for him to follow. All the ease that had come over her earlier was gone. She felt sapped off energy. She just wanted to go home, though sleep and bed held no appeal.

She waited on the sidewalk for Mac to join her. "I want to thank you for the evening," she said formally. "And for at least going in there." She glanced at him, then away. "Good-bye, detective." She turned to walk away.

"Hey, where are you going?" He caught her arm, pulling her around.

"Home." She looked pointedly down at the hand on her arm.

"When I take a woman out to dinner, I see her to her door," he said.

"That's not necessary, especially when you took her out to dinner to decide if she was a psychotic killer. Can I ask you, why didn't you detain me earlier if I knew too much about how the woman was killed?"

"Because the woman was about the same height as you and the entry wound was at a downward angle. The killer had to be someone who was taller."

"I guess that's good. So I'm not a suspect."

"That's right, now will you let me take you home?" He motioned to the car.

"It's only a couple of blocks."

"I know, and I'll see you there and walk you up to your apartment."

From the look in his eyes, she knew he wasn't going to give up, so she let him turn her toward the car.

Ten minutes later Laken closed the door on Detective MacDaniels and let out a sigh. Life just wasn't fair. She got double-crossed by her boss, and now the most interesting man she'd met in her life thought she's either a liar or psychotic or a psychotic liar. "Just great." She ambled through her small apartment and wondered for the umpteenth time that day if she really wanted to live there anymore.

Deciding she really didn't want to face those thoughts again, she headed for the bedroom. The sight of the bed made her pause. Did she really want to try to sleep? With the possibility of dreams waiting, the answer was a resounding 'no' but after several games of solitaire and seventy-five pages of the book she'd been wanting to read, she slid into sleep. Luckily, The Hunter was not on the prowl.

Chapter Four

Mac couldn't believe he was in the library to do research on dreams and psychics on his Saturday off. The image of Laken came to his mind, not that she'd been far from his thoughts. She had been in his dreams. He turned down the row where the numbers of the books that he wanted were to be found and the picture in his mind took form in a living breathing woman.

"Laken." Her name escaped him in a rush of air and she turned to him, obviously startled. Color flared in her cheeks. She looked embarrassed. He glanced at the numbers beside her, then back to her. "It seems like we have the same thoughts."

"I wanted to figure out what happened to me. To explain, to try to ... why are you here?"

"Looking for explanations."

The look in her eyes said he'd shocked her. A smile spread across her lips. "You were going to check it out."

"Dreams and visions. I decided it wouldn't hurt to take a look."

"Thank you." Her look would've been worthy of slaying a dragon.

"I haven't done anything yet."

"Yes, you did. You came to check it out, even though it goes against what you believe. You're giving me a chance."

He felt oddly embarrassed and greatly pleased. "So what have you found so far?"

"I just got here and was just going to pull books." She held out a paper that listed many of the same numbers on his paper. Together they gathered the books and headed to an empty table away from other people.

An hour and a half later, he was fascinated and frustrated. There was no proof but a lot of belief, myths and legends of people moving through dreams, and others of people near death leaving their body. The scariest thing about that was the thought of Laken being that near gone. Mac didn't know what to believe but it was obvious Laken believed what she dreamt was the truth.

Across the table, he heard the book close and drop to the table. He closed his own and looked over to her. "Well?"

"I don't know what to think," she said, frustrated.

"Ditto."

"So what do we do now?" She looked to him, her beautiful green eyes burned with unanswered questions.

"I say we go for lunch and then to the zoo."

"The zoo?" The surprise on her face was gratifying.

"Yeah, I like the zoo. It's a good place to think. Walk, talk, and get to know each other. It's a nice day out there. Or, what about baseball? Do you like baseball?"

She started to laugh, a totally uninhibited sound. "I take it you like baseball."

"I don't like to watch it on TV. It's a kind of have to be there thing. But I always enjoy a good game, to play or watch if I'm there. I have the weekend off, and I think you're in for some free time to enjoy yourself. What do you say baseball today, zoo tomorrow? I'll even buy you a hotdog. Do you think you'd enjoy being with me?"

"Yes." The word slid out of her.

"Then baseball?"

"Yes."

They spent the rest of the day, and late into the evening, laughing and cheering since the game went into extra innings. Mac dropped her off at her apartment leaving them both in better moods than the night before. The next morning, he was there at nine o'clock to get her.

They stopped for breakfast on the way to the zoo. By the time they made it to the monkey cages, they were holding hands and talking freely of everything they could think of that didn't involve murder and visions. The only dreams that came into the conversation were those of the future.

Laken told him of wanting to move out of the city and have a house with a yard. She wanted to make a go of it on her own, but she was afraid of not being able to compete with the larger firms. She told him of her family and growing up. That she had an older sister who was married, a brother who was an engineer, and another who was a pilot in the Air Force. She was the youngest.

He told her how he always wanted to be a police officer. After the zoo, they stopped for dinner.

"I feel guilty letting you pay all the time," Laken said as they left the restaurant. It was late, dark outside. Cars filled the street with people coming and going.

"You can buy next time." He tugged her tight to his side.

"I'll tell you what. How about I fix you dinner tomorrow? That is if you don't have to work or have other plans."

"I'm on from six to four."

"Then I'll plan dinner about six," she said easily. "That should give me enough time after work to throw something together."

"I'll bring a movie. Any special requests?"

"Just nothing sad."

"I have a thing for comedies or adventure."

"Either work for me." She smiled.

"Then we have a date."

"I thought we were on a date right now." They reached

his car and she turned back to face him.

He looked thoughtful. "True, but I haven't got to kiss you – yet."

"Is that what it takes to be a date?"

He wasn't sure if she was teasing or encouraging him, but he knew how he was taking it. He moved closer, pinning her between him and the car. "I'm thinking it could help," he murmured just before his lips came down to brush hers. They caught and held.

A groan of pleasure escaped Laken, and he tightened his hold. Her arm made it up around his neck and the kiss continued until a distant horn invaded Mac's mind and he realized they were standing in the street.

The woman in his arms looked dazed and utterly adorable. "I think that makes this a date," he said satisfied.

"I'd say so."

He kissed her again at the door a few minutes later, this time careful of the electricity that seemed to combust between them, he kept it brief. He whistled his way back down to his car, the image of Laken on his mind.

That was how a man should spend his weekend. With a beautiful woman who was intelligent and intriguing. And he had a date tomorrow night for a home cooked meal. Life was looking pretty good. It'd be great if they didn't have her visions of murder and him with a victim that really fit them. There was still going to be more to deal with, though he decided tomorrow was soon enough to handle it.

Cง฿ว

"So how was the weekend off? I was almost expecting you to show up here," Jonesy greeted Mac as he settled at his desk.

"I was busy. I had a date."

"What, hey, when did this happen? You were moaning the state of your social life when you left."

"It's picked up since."

"Oh, really." He moved over to sit on the edge of

Mac's desk. "So who's the woman?"

"Laken Williams."

"Laken, wait a minute, the fruitcake?"

"She's not a fruitcake," Mac shot back.

"Okay, you want to say liar," Jonesy challenged.

"She's not lying."

"Don't tell me you believe her now." His friend arched his eyebrow at him. "That must have been some date. That's not what you were thinking on Friday."

"Don't be going there, that's not what happened. Laken believes everything she told us." Mac went on to explain finding her at the park then at the library.

"I don't think you should be going out with her. She's involved with this case. Somehow, she knows way too much about that murder. Mac, she said that the killer stepped on the victim. I haven't been able to get that out of my mind. How could she know that?"

"I don't know. I can't explain it and neither can she. I believe her, Marcus." Mac used his partner's given name for emphasis.

"Well, you better come up with something better than that. I respect your instinct but so far, she's the closest thing we have to a suspect." He looked back pointedly.

Mac felt his stomach clench. "You can't be serious about that."

Jonesy's eyebrow cocked up to say he was totally serious.

"What about the angle of the knife?" It was Mac's turn to point out.

"You put her in heels and she'd about be the right height if she was reaching up over her shoulder. She also lives only a couple blocks from where we found the body."

"There is no way she would have the strength to hold the victim that close to reach around her back and stab her without the evidence of a struggle on either of them," Mac shot back.

"What if she was giving her a hug? There are women who do that huggy-kissy thing. And we kind of wrote off the jealous lover angle, but we didn't really consider a female too strongly as a possibility because the neighbors said, she was into guys."

"You're now saying Laken was her lover."

"It's just speculation."

"No way." Mac slammed his hand on the desk.

"Why, because she went out with you? It'd be a good way to throw you off," Jonesy challenged.

"Then why come forward in the first place?"

"I don't know? Maybe she wanted to find out what we knew, maybe get a thrill, like an arsonist watching his own fire."

"You're stretching it, pal."

"You're the one stretching it getting involved with someone from a case. You've never done that before."

The genuine concern in Jonesy's voice tempered the anger rising in Mac. He hated any discord between them. It wasn't uncommon for them to play devil's advocate off each other many times, but this was different – this involved Laken. And something in Mac cried out she was special to him, even though he was just getting to know her.

"Hayes and Mikey ran a check on her."

Jonesy's comment pulled him out the reverie he'd slipped into. Mac wanted to object to them running a check, but he originally planned on doing one himself. "What'd they find?"

"She came back clean, I mean totally clean. The woman hasn't even had a ticket in her life. How can you live here and not get a ticket? How can you live anywhere and not get a ticket? She's just too squeaky clean. We think we should bring her in."

The satisfaction Mac was feeling switched to sickness on Jonesy's last comment. "You want to bring her in to interrogate her because she's squeaky clean."

"I think we'd better think about it. You'd better think about it, and you'd better think about canceling your date with her, or you're going to end up with a big conflict of interest."

Mac stared at his partner feeling like his world had shattered much like it did when he woke up in the hospital.

❧

"I can call you when he gets in, Laken," Kathy suggested for the third time.

Laken shook her head. She'd already been waiting outside Stewart Hoster's office for nearly forty minutes and wasn't about to give up. "I'm afraid that he'll just sneak in and say he doesn't want to be disturbed. I want my questions answered."

There was a sympathetic look on the secretary's face, and she didn't try to suggest it wouldn't happen. Both women knew the man would do just that.

Laken pulled out another set of specs she needed to go over and started to check the figures. Another five minutes passed before Hoster burst through the door, dressed in his normal pristine suit with a handkerchief sticking out the pocket that matched his tie. He had Laken by five inches in height and fifty pounds in weight but Laken stood up right in his path.

"What are you doing here? You should be at work." Hoster snapped, obviously not pleased to see her.

"I have been working, but I need to talk to you."

"Well, I'm busy now. It'll have to wait." He went to move around her.

Laken stepped in his way, too annoyed at the way she was being treated to worry about how her boss felt. "I need to talk to you, now. I won't to be put off any longer."

A glint of what might be fury crossed the man's face. "Oh, all right. I'll give you five minutes." He turned into his office, leaving her to follow.

Hoster moved around his desk and dropped into his leather chair. "Now, what is it?"

"I want to know why I was left out of the meeting on Thursday."

"You were sick," he said simply and made a motion as if waving her away.

"I wasn't sick when you initially told me the time of the meeting."

"You must've written it wrong."

"No, I didn't." Laken stepped forward placing her hands on the desk, leaning forward in challenge. "You told me one o'clock several times, and I checked to know it wasn't rescheduled. You told me the wrong time. And, you did it on purpose."

"What are you so upset about? Your plans got presented. I did it myself. So what's the problem? If they are chosen, you will get the bonus. So quit worrying about it and get back to work," he retorted dismissively.

"But why did you leave me out of the meeting?"

"You were sick. You shouldn't have been there," he restated. "Now get back to work. Unless you want to be fired," the man barked out red faced.

Laken couldn't believe what he'd said, fired. She almost opened her mouth to say she didn't care. She just wanted an answer but, at the last second, caught herself. She couldn't afford to get fired, at least, not until she made some decisions. Besides, it wouldn't look good for her to be fired. Holding her anger in, she stormed out of the office.

Hours later, Laken still fumed. She couldn't believe it, he wouldn't give her an answer why, and then he had actually threatened to fire her. She stared at the blueprint she was going over, not really seeing it. What was going on in her life?

The phone rang behind her. She automatically turned to grab it. "I wanted to give you a heads up," Kathy's voice

said hurriedly. "The police are on the way back to see you."
The line went dead in her ear.

Police. Mac was here. A surge of pleasure went
through her. Life was not totally bad, she smiled and
turned. Her smile faded and she started to rethink her last
thought when she caught the grim look on his face and the
sternness on his partner's.

"Miss Williams." It was his partner that spoke first.
Mac sent his partner a glare but let him continue. "We'd
like to ask you some questions."

"Laken, is there somewhere we can speak privately?"
Mac added quietly.

She turned her attention fully to him, trying to see the
man she'd spent the weekend at the library, ball game, and
zoo with. A cold exterior covered him like a shield. This
was the man that handled the darker side of life. Unable to
get words out, she nodded, leading them down the hall to
the conference room. Fortunately, it was empty.

"What is it?" Laken couldn't keep back the question
any longer. Fear flooded over her. "Did he kill again?"

"No," Mac said gently. "We need you to go over
everything you told us the other day again."

"Okay." Her discomfort rising at the tone in his voice.

"We'd like to record it if you don't mind." Detective
Jones stepped forward pulling a tape recorder from his
pocket, putting it on the table, he then motioned her to the
chair in front of it.

Her legs trembled as she stepped to the chair and
dropped into it.

"You don't have to do this, Laken." Mac spoke from
where he stood just inside the door. She looked back at him
and he continued. "You can also have an attorney present if
you'd like."

"Am I in trouble?"

"No, ma'am," Jones answered, but she didn't look at
him.

"Mac?"

"No," he let out, but she could tell he didn't like his answer. She didn't think he was lying though.

"Okay." She waited while they got settled and Detective Jones said the date and her name into the recorder then announced that she declined wanting an attorney present.

With that finished he asked her to repeat what she had told them on Friday, stopping her several times to repeat or clarify what she said. The whole time Mac stood stoically to the side, leaning against the wall. A grime expression on his face.

Finally, after going though it a second time, Laken couldn't take it anymore. "That's enough. You don't believe me. Why are you doing this?" She turned on Mac. "Say something, Mac."

He raised his head when she cried out his name and reached out to turn off the recorder. "It's better I don't."

"Why?"

He glanced toward the other man and glared. "Because it could compromise the case."

"I don't understand. How could it affect the case? I'm not..." She froze. "But, you said I wasn't a suspect. That I was too short for the angle of the knife."

He grimaced at her comment.

"You believe." Laken felt tears pool in her eyes but refused to let them fall. "You think I killed her."

That got to him. "No." He stepped away from the wall his hand going out to her, but he stopped before reaching her.

Using all the control she had, she stood, head held high. "No, you just believe I'm a liar." She turned to Detective Jones. "You think I'm guilty. You just can't figure out how to pin it on me. We're done here. I need to get back to work."

"Laken." Mac reached to take her hand as she started

to move passed him.

She jerked back, pain crushing down on her. "No! Don't come near me again." She swung from him going the long way around the table.

"Laken, I don't believe you're lying."

She paused with her hand on the door handle. "Funny, I believe you do. Good-bye, Mac." She left the men in the room. Instead of going back to her cubby to work, she kept going down the hall to the ladies room. Since her and Kathy were the only females on that floor she had it to herself to let the tears flow.

Chapter Five

Mac watched Laken go, aching to go after her as he'd yearned to hold her for the last hour.

"Mac."

He turned on Jones, wanting to plow his fist into his partner. "Don't say anything," he snarled.

"Let it go."

"I did let it go." The image of Laken burned in his mind in stark clarity – a picture of pain and betrayal. "And, I'm beginning to feel just what I lost."

"Come on, man, get serious."

He looked to the man who had been his best friend for four years. "I'm totally serious. And you know what? After just sitting here, and doing nothing while I let you grill her, I deserve to lose her."

He left his partner to follow him. He wasn't surprised not to see Laken at her work area when he looked. Resigned, he stepped into the elevator.

He started calling her cell phone when he got to his car. She didn't answer. At the station, he called again. It clicked off on him. The next time, he called it went directly to messaging. She'd turned off her cell phone.

CZ80

Laken was miserable. With each minute, her emotions swung between hurt and anger. How in just a couple days had Spencer MacDaniels come to mean so much to her? She fought back a wave of tears. The arrogant jerk. She didn't need him. She stomped her way up the stairs. She'd just reached her apartment when the door across the hall opened.

"Oh, Laken. I thought I heard someone out here but wasn't sure it was you. You usually move around so quietly."

Laken plastered a smile on her face and turned to the woman. Mrs. Simmons was a nice, old, busybody, who dyed her hair an unfortunate shade of orange and was always coming up with reasons to visit. Laken would have enjoyed her visits more if she just wasn't so pushy.

"How are you tonight, Mrs. Simmons?" she asked, not wanting to start a conversation but knowing it was the fastest way to escape.

"Oh, just wonderful, dear, my nephew is here to visit. Howard, you know. You promised the next time he was in town you'd go out with him."

Laken groaned inwardly. This couldn't be happening, now. "I'm sorry, Mrs. Simmons, but I had a really miserable day at work. I don't think I'd be very good company tonight."

"Nonsense. A night out is just what you need."

"It really isn't a good time."

"Pish-posh." The woman waved her hand. "Now, dear, I've told Howard all about you. He's anxious to meet you. He's at a meeting now but will be back about six-thirty. I think that by seven he should have time to get ready."

"I should stay home. You know I was sick last week."

"He's planning on picking you up then," the woman continued as if Laken hadn't said anything. Laken resigned herself to go out. At least, she could get it over with, and the woman wouldn't be after her forever. And, who knew, maybe Howard would be as wonderful as Mrs. Simmons made him out to be, and she could forget about an infuriating broad-shouldered detective.

CBEO

On the way home from work, Mac stopped at the

pharmacy. Fortunately, one of the clerks from the night of the murder was there. Mac introduced himself and showed his badge. "I was wondering if you might be able to remember a couple of customers that were in here last Wednesday."

"I help a lot of people," the man said. "But, you say Wednesday. That's the night it rained so hard."

"Yes," Mac confirmed, feeling a surge of hope.

"We weren't too busy. People stayed in because of the rain." The man was obviously thinking back.

"I'm interested in two women. Both about five-eight with light brown hair, the first one was sick."

"Oh, yeah, I remember her. She was real sick. It was amazing she could even stand up. I wondered if I shouldn't call an ambulance she looked so bad. Nothing happened to her, did it? I've seen her around. She's usually nice and friendly. She said she was going right home to bed. That she'd be fine," he added.

"No, she's fine. The other woman that I'm wondering about was in here at the same time."

The man thought a minute. "Oh yeah, the promotion girl."

"Promotion?"

"Yeah, she was bragging how she'd just got a big promotion. Won out big over everyone else. She was going to plan a celebration for the weekend, but just had to tell someone right then."

"You don't happen to have her name do you?"

The man looked hesitant.

"It could be important," Mac stressed.

"Well, I remember she bought some things using her credit card."

"Great, I don't want to get you into any trouble, but could you just check and see if her name was Andrea Chambers by chance."

"I guess that would be okay just to confirm it." He

went to the office and came back a few minutes later. "That's the name all right. Does that help?"

"Yes, it does, thank you. One other thing, do you happen to remember a man in here at that same time? He was wearing a dark raincoat."

"Yeah, a black one, with a hat pulled down low. I remember him." The clerk stated firmly. "I kept a close eye on him. I was afraid he might be going to rob the place, after drugs and cash."

"Can you describe him?"

"Not more then what you just said. He kept his face turned away so I never got a look at his face. That was one of the reasons I thought he might be going to rob us. He didn't ever come close to the counter. Didn't buy a thing. Just walked up and down the aisle, stopping every once-in-awhile. I was real relieved when he left, believe me."

"When was that, before or after the women?"

"Oh man, I'm not sure. I think it was after one of them, but I don't know."

"What about video surveillance." Mac motioned to the camera fixed to the ceiling.

"It runs for a week then is recycled. You'd have to talk to the owner."

"Can you get me the number? I need the tape from that night."

The man nodded and a second later handed him the number. Mac walked out of the pharmacy with the video in hand and only one thing on his mind – and that was seeing Laken. Since his car was parked halfway there, he didn't bother with it. He took the stairs to her apartment and knocked. When there was no answer, he knocked again. By the third time he knocked, he was getting annoyed.

"Come on, Laken. Open up, it's Mac. I need to talk to you, it's important. Laken!" He raised his voice just as the door across the hall opened, an old woman with tightly curled, orange hair peered in the hallway.

"Excuse me, ma'am. I'm sorry if I interrupted you."

The woman looked him up and down then opened the door wider. "She's not home. She's on a date."

"A date?" Mac felt the shock hit him like a fist in the stomach.

"Oh yes, they made a splendid looking couple. I knew they would be perfect together."

"Pardon me, but I'm Detective MacDaniels, I really need to talk to Ms. Williams. Do you have any idea when she'll be back?"

"Oh, I expect quite late. You being a young man yourself, you can understand that."

Mac couldn't believe the woman actually gave him a conspiratorial wink.

"Is there anything I can do for you?" the woman volunteered.

"I'm afraid not. Ms. Williams is involved in a case I'm working on."

"Oh really. What kind of case?"

"I'm a homicide detective."

The woman looked shocked to near apoplexy.

"If you happen to see her, could you have Ms. Williams call me when she gets in?"

"Of course."

Mac hated to leave but knew there was no reason to stay. It was unlikely that Laken would have anything to do with him. Not giving the woman a chance to say anything else, he headed for the stairs. Since there was no way he was going to get his home cooked meal, he decided to head back to the station to pull a late nighter going over the surveillance video with the lab people.

It was late when he got home. Not that it mattered. There was no one there waiting for him. Mac stretched out on the bed, thinking of the woman who hadn't left his thoughts since meeting her.

He would never in his life forget how broken she

looked when she left the conference room. It would burn in his soul the rest of his life. He wished there was a way he could make it better, but she wouldn't even answer her phone to let him try. The thought of her on a date with another man ate at him.

She'd said she wasn't dating anyone. He replayed the conversation with her neighbor over in his mind. It sounded like they hadn't been dating long. The woman said what – that they made a splendid looking couple. That she knew they would. Had she set them up on the date or was it wishful thinking on his part?

Mac wanted to bang his head against the wall in frustration. Laken should have been out with him.

Well, now he had the proof that at least part of what Laken told them was the truth. He had the record that the victim had been in the pharmacy, and the video that showed them both. Unfortunately, there were only brief glimpses of the man in the raincoat, and none clear enough to pull a description from. But he was just as Laken described. The question was how to prove the other part. There didn't seem any way.

Hypnosis, the thought hit him so strong he sat up in bed. What would happen if they hypnotized Laken? Then if she had seen it some way it would come out or if someone told her, they could learn that to.

The question was, after what happened earlier that day, if she would agree to be hypnotized. Well, for that he had a trump card. Laken's conscience would have her do anything to help them stop the killer before he struck again.

෴

Laken stepped to her door in relief. Her hand was already locked on her keys. The evening was pretty much how she feared. Howard was decent looking, a little over six feet tall, but there was a nerdy, mama's boy-look about him that irritated her from the beginning. That, and the way he kept eyeing her like she was a new toy. And, if he looked down at her bust one more time, she would smack him.

She'd purposely dressed conservatively, with a high neck sweater that didn't hug her body and a long skirt with her boots. She was literally covered head to toe, but it didn't seem to shield her from Howard's roaming eyes.

Conversation was just as bad. He'd talked incessantly about himself. His accomplishments in his job and superiority over all the fools and idiots that he was forced to work with. Laken wondered if she was supposed to gush over his brilliance, but he seemed too busy doing it himself to notice she wasn't.

She unlocked the door and turned back to him. "Well, thank you for the nice evening."

He stepped close and started to lean over her. Laken put up a hand to hold him off. He looked almost comically confused.

"I thought that I'd come in for a while." His voice hummed with meaning that irritated Laken.

"I'm sorry, Howard. I'm very of tired and want to go straight to bed."

"That's fine with me." His look was leering.

Laken was shocked, and felt her ire rising. "That was not an invitation."

This time the man looked taken back. "What is this, we went out to dinner and that little club for music?"

"Yes and that is all that is happening."

"What's going on? Aunt Ardith said you don't date much."

"Not a lot. What does that have to do with you coming in?" Her anger stepped up a notch.

"Well, you should be happy to get a little."

"A little? As in you going to bed with me? No!" She really couldn't believe he was serious, but there was no doubt he was.

"What do you mean, no. I bought you dinner."

"Yes, but that doesn't mean you bought me."

"I thought—"

"You thought wrong. Here." She pulled the money she kept in her pocket in case of emergency during a date out and shoved it at him. "That should cover my dinner."

"That's not half."

"But it's more than enough for my dinner, and I'm not going to pay for all the wine you drank and I didn't. Good-bye, Howard." She stepped through the door and closed it in his face. Barely catching his remark, "No wonder she doesn't date, tight—"

Laken sank back against the door. What a miserable night. Correction – what a miserable day. Could her life get any worse?

Chapter Six

Laken forced herself to concentrate on the wall section she was moving to make room for the change in the ventilation system that the owner opted for. Usually, details like this really didn't bother her too much. They just seemed silly that it wasn't decided in the first place, but today, she could just scream with frustration. Today, she could scream about a lot, mainly deceitful men and underhanded bosses, which were one and the same in her book.

"Miss Williams." The voice from one of the top people on her annoyance list called her name.

She turned, not bothering to hold back completely the glare at her boss. "Yes, Mr. Hoster."

The man looked decisively unfriendly, which was okay, because she was still not very happy with him. "I heard that the police were here questioning you yesterday. I want to know what that was about."

Great! That was all she needed, she groaned under her breath. "It was nothing, sir." She hated that he expected the title, unless of course, you were one of his golfing buddies.

"I heard they stayed quite some time and that you were quite upset when they left." He stared down at her in his patented disapproving look, that she didn't realize until then, really annoyed her.

"There's a case they are working on that I have some information about. They came to go back over my statement and to see if I remembered any other details."

She figured that was pretty much the truth.

"What kind of a case?"

"I don't think I'm allowed to talk about it. It's still under investigation, and they're keeping information back for the time being." She could tell the man didn't like her answer, though he couldn't say anything to object. Laken found herself taking pleasure in the fact. It wasn't like her to be ornery, but between the lack of sleep, nightmares plaguing what sleep she did get, and the way she'd been treated, she had just a little too much in the last couple days to feel guilty.

"Miss Williams, if you are involved in anything illegal, I will be forced to let you go." The man huffed at her.

"What?" She couldn't believe what he'd said. "Mr. Hoster, I witnessed something. Surely you can't hold that against me."

"If it affects your job or the image of this firm, it can't be tolerated."

Laken couldn't believe him, then it hit her – he was looking for any excuse to fire her. But why? She did good work. She carried more than her fair share of the workload assigned in the drafting group.

"Mr. Hoster, it is not affecting the performance of my job, and I have put in plenty of extra time to cover the time that I talked to them. I have a sound work ethic. I am reliable. I feel strongly about doing my best for the company, and feel I do so. I had some information on a crime, so I went to the police about it. I felt it was my duty. That is it. It will not affect my work."

"See that it doesn't." The intercom sounded, ruining his snide comment.

Laken ignored it to return his gaze until it sounded again. She reached over and pushed the button. "Laken, there is a Detective MacDaniels on line three, says he's been trying to get hold of you, that it's important." Laken was tempted to tell Kathy to disconnect it but couldn't with

Hoster standing there.

"Was there anything else?" She hoped the man would move away but no such luck. Laken grabbed up the phone, giving her normal greeting.

"Don't hang up." Mac's voice rushed out at her over the phone. Still, she might have slammed down the phone if Hoster wasn't staring down at her.

"What may I do for you, detective?" She enunciated every syllable, forcing herself to sound civil.

"Please, listen, I'm sorry. I couldn't get involved in the interview. But I do believe you. I've checked out the pharmacy. The clerk remembered all of you, and I have the video. Unfortunately there no clear shot of the guy."

He rushed the words out, as if he was afraid she'd hang up on him, but he had her right after 'I believe you'.

"I think I've come up with an idea to help convince the other detectives to take you seriously. Would you be willing to be hypnotized? I think it might help, and you might be able to remember more details." He finally stopped talking, letting the words hang.

Laken was too shocked to answer. He had checked out the pharmacy. Hypnotized? She could only stare at her boss's disapproving frown.

"Laken?" Mac called her over the phone. "Are you still there?"

"Yes."

"I have an appointment with the force psychologist at four-thirty. Can you make that?" The hope in his voice was clear to her.

"Yes," she let the word out slowly.

"Good, I'll be there to get you just after four."

"No," Laken shot back, feeling a stab of pain. Even if he did believe her, she wasn't ready to give into him that far yet. "I'll get there on my own. What's the address?" She turned her back on her boss to write it down. "I'll be there." She disconnected.

When she looked back, Hoster still glared down at her and then turned away without further comment.

လၢၗ

Laken's stomach clenched again as she stepped off the elevator. What she couldn't tell was if it was fear of being hypnotized or seeing Mac again that was making her nervous. She didn't get a chance to decide before he was there in front of her.

"Laken." He said her name like a starving man savoring a feast.

She wanted to turn away but was frozen in place, drinking up the sight of him. Pain rose again. Her hand came up to hold back the sob that came with it. Before it could escape, Mac crossed the distance between them and wrapped his arms around her, pulling her to his chest.

"I'm so sorry." There was a tremor to his words. His lips brushed her temple, as he buried his face into her hair. "Please, forgive me?"

Unable to stop herself, Laken slipped her arms around him, amazed at how right the action felt. She breathed in the clean musky smell that was Mac. Behind them someone cleared their throat. "Detective MacDaniels, Dr. Shannon is ready for you now."

Mac leaned back and framed her face with his hands. "Are you okay with this?"

Laken was comforted by the concern in his eyes. "Yes," she managed to squeeze out past her throat that had suddenly gone dry. "Will you be with me?"

"Right by you," he promised, bringing her hand to his lips, kissing her fingers before interlocking them with his to lead her into the room.

A small, compact woman, who Laken guessed to be in her mid-fifties, stood as they entered the room. "Mac," the woman greeted him then turned to her. "You must be Miss Williams."

"Call me Laken, please." Laken extended her hand to

shake the woman's.

"Thank you, I'm Laura. I prefer being on a first name basis. It tends to make people feel more comfortable. Won't you sit down?" She directed them to a sitting area with a suede-leather couch, a coffee table and two wing-back chairs. "Would you like something to drink?"

"Could I have some water please?"

"Of course. Please, I need you relaxed if I'm going to hypnotize you. You are willing?"

"Yes. Just a little nervous."

"That's understandable, but there's nothing to be worried about." The woman poured a couple glasses then settled down in a chair while Laken sat beside Mac on the couch. "Mac has told me a little about what happened with you. I have to admit, I'm quite fascinated. There is much to be learned about the dream state."

Laken glanced up at Mac then back to her. "You believe me then?"

"Oh, yes. Though I have to admit I have never dealt with anything quite like what you experienced. I've been trying to decide the best way to go about this. If I should have you tell me about the dream first, or just go into it with you under hypnosis. I've decided to have you tell me all you can remember, so I can know better what to ask. Is that okay with you?"

"Yes."

"Good, before we start, Mac asked if it was okay if we record the sessions."

Laken cleared her throat. "It's fine."

"All right. Why don't you tell me about that night?"

By now, Laken had gone over it so many times it no longer threatened to overwhelm her. Eventually they switched to just talking.

Mac kept his free hand moving over Laken's arm in what he hoped was a soothing fashion. He hated to see Laken forced to bring up the terrible images again. He was proud of the way she handled it, and realized how strong she was. Even facing certain disbelief, she had come forward to help. His heart swelled as he looked down at her fingers still interlocked with his.

It took all his will power not to drag her out of there, to a place where she never had to face the bad things in life again. He relaxed along with Laken when the story ended. He then watched as Dr. Shannon directed her in relaxing further. Just listening to the woman's voice, Laken seemed to slip into sleep.

"Is she all right?" Mac could no longer keep from asking when Dr. Shannon stepped forward to check her.

"Oh, yes. Let's get started. Laken can you hear me?"

"Yes," her voice was soft, kind of dreamy.

"Good, I would like you to go back to last Wednesday."

Laken shook her head. "I don't feel good. I wish I had something to make me feel better. I need to finish the last changes done to my plans. Hoster's demanding that I work the Christensen's plans. I don't know why. They aren't due for two weeks, and they're supposed to be Jeff's assignment."

"Good, can you go later, after work?"

"Almost done, just have to print the sheet with the new changes. So sick. I just want to sleep, but I'm done. They are perfect, so perfect. Feel awful. Maybe I should just get a little sleep before I try to go home. No, if I go to sleep I won't make it home, and I won't get medicine. I have to get some medicine, go home and sleep. Just want to sleep."

"It's so cold. I'm so hot. I hate being sick. I can't believe I forgot my umbrella. I don't like to wait for the bus alone when it's dark, but it should be here soon. I feel so awful. Need some medicine."

She moved restlessly.

"It is okay, Laken. You're not sick anymore. Do you understand?"

"Yes."

"Good, can you tell me about the woman at the pharmacy?"

Mac leaned forward, listening to her repeat pretty much what she'd told him before, but this time going into the conversation she'd overheard.

"That was very good. Laken, I need you to tell me about the man now in the raincoat."

Calmly again, she told everything that happened in the pharmacy. Mac experienced a wave of rage when she repeated how the man had touched her then licked his finger. Dr. Shannon led her through the dream. They were just finishing when Laken jerked and shivered, the violence of her action taking him by surprise.

"It's okay, Laken." Dr. Shannon stood and moved to her.

"No," she cried out.

"She's getting hot." Mac moved a hand to her forehead alarmed. "She's burning up."

"Laken, it's all right."

"No, he's angry. It's building. He's going to hunt. He's going to. He'll teach them. They are nothing. Shouldn't be let out of the house. They forget their place."

"Who, Laken?

Laken shook her head back and forth as if trying to fight off the answer. "He's going to hunt." Her words came in raspy gasps.

"Laken, can you tell me his name."

She shook her head.

"Can you describe him?"

Again, she began to shake her head. "He's in a crowded room. There's so much noise. It's buzzing in his head. It's not fair. How can they think to compete with him? They are weak. He is stronger, smarter, better. They are nothing." She cried out in pain. Her breathing labored.

Her skin was so hot Mac could hardly touch her.

"We've got to bring her out of this," he demanded, feeling his own panic.

"Yes," Dr. Shannon agreed her own worry plain to see. "Laken, Laken can you hear me?" There was no response.

"Laken," Mac couldn't keep from calling her name. She jerked.

"That's it," Dr. Shannon said. "Laken, it's okay. Mac's here, he has you. Hold her tight, talk to her."

"Laken, sweetheart, listen to me, I'm here. I have you. I won't let anything hurt you."

"He's going to kill again," Laken cried out.

"Come on, sweetheart, I have you. I'm right here. You're safe. You need to listen to Laura."

"Laken, you're going to relax now. Everything is all right. You are going to feel better now. When you wake up, the dream won't plague you. You'll remember last Wednesday clearly, but you will not be afraid. He can't reach you. Do you hear me?"

"Yes." Her breathing smoothed and became regular. Her body temperature fell to normal. She let out a huge sigh. A shiver of released tension shook her, then she stilled, calm in Mac's arms.

"Very good, Laken, now, I'm going to count to three, and you will wake up. One, two, three."

Mac let out a sigh of his own when Laken opened her eyes. She looked up at him holding her to him with one arm. His other hand still held hers, their fingers interlocked. "Welcome back." He smiled down, never so happy in his life.

"Did it work?" She looked at him then to the doctor.

"Yes," she said smoothly. "You remembered a few more details, but it was all pretty much the same. How do you feel?"

"Okay, just a little tired and thirsty."

Mac reached for her glass. "Here."

She took it and drained what was left, and Dr. Shannon refilled it for her to drink again. "Thank you. I'm so thirsty."

Mac exchanged looks with Dr. Shannon.

"That's understandable. You did very well."

"What do you think?" Laken looked hopeful for answers.

"I will tell you. I found it very fascinating. I'd like to go over the tape before I comment more on it. Then, if you don't mind, I'd like to see you again."

"You don't think I lied then or am making it up?" Yearning rang in her voice.

"No. I will try to find some answers for you," the doctor said soothingly.

The words seemed to help Laken relax. "Thank you." Laken glanced at her watch and looked startled. "Oh, my, I didn't realize it was so late."

Mac glanced at his own watch. An hour and a half had passed.

"That was why I had you as my last appointment. I hope that it's okay?" Dr. Shannon smiled unconcerned.

"Yes, I just didn't realize that much time passed."

"I understand." The doctor rose with them, going to the door. They were through it when Dr. Shannon said. "Mac, can I speak to you alone for a minute, please?" The woman looked thoughtful.

"I'll just be a minute." He looked down at Laken. "Wait for me, please." He waited until she nodded before going back in the office. When Dr. Shannon closed the door behind him, he turned to her. "Yes?"

The doctor seemed to take a second to collect her thoughts. "I wanted to tell you that I believe everything she said. I'm quite concerned about Laken's fever. The thing is, it shouldn't have happened. It was extremely high, too high to be healthy for a person. I can't explain it, but I think it's a link."

"A link to what?"

"I'm not sure. As I said before, I'll have to do some research and see if I can find anything out."

The sense of dread slipped back into him, but all Mac could do was nod. He was relieved to see Laken waiting for him when he opened the door. A smile crept to her lips and pleasure filled him. She wasn't mad at him anymore. Everything would be all right. He moved directly in front of her, so her head had to tip up to look at him. Her fingers locked around his as he took her hand.

"Would you like to go get something to eat?" He raised his other hand to brush back the hair from her chin. Her skin was incredibly soft. He longed to caress it, to cup her face and draw her to him. And, since the room was empty, he did just that.

She met the kiss, giving herself over to him. When the kiss ended, he pulled her to him, her head coming down to rest on his chest. "This is how it should be between us." He brushed his lips across her forehead.

"Yes." She nuzzled tighter and sighed.

"Hey," he said after a minute, "Are you going to sleep on me?"

He felt her sigh again. "Maybe. It feels so good to be in your arms, and I'm so very tired."

"Late night?" He winced at his own question but couldn't help asking it.

"Awful night. First it was what happened with us. Then, I got to my apartment, and my neighbor caught me. She's been trying to set me up with her nephew, and he was in town." Laken shuddered and tightened her hold on him.

"That bad?"

"Yes."

He kissed the top of her head, and she relaxed again. He felt a small yawn slip from her. "I don't think I'll make it going out to dinner." There was a definite sleepiness in her words.

"Tell you what. I know a place that has great soup. How about we get a couple bowls to go? And then I'll take you home and we'll eat there."

She leaned back and looked up at him. "That sounds perfect. There's a bakery on my street that makes wonderful breads. We can grab a loaf on the way up."

An hour later, Laken sat curled up on the couch, her head resting against Mac's shoulder. His arms wrapped around her. She felt warm, happy and totally content.

"I think you're falling asleep on me again." The words rumbled under her ear.

"Yes." She tilted her head to place a kiss against his neck, the arm around her tightened. She smiled and pressed another kiss to his skin.

"Oh, sweetheart." He groaned.

She watched his Adam's apple bob up and down. Without thought, her finger came up to trace it. He was so fascinating.

His hand came up to catch hers bringing it up to his lips.

She tilted her head up to find him looking down at her. "Sorry," she whispered, feeling embarrassed by her forwardness.

"You have nothing to be sorry for," he fairly growled out. "I'm just trying to be noble here. You've had a lot of upheaval in your life lately. You're tired and need rest. And, well, I find you extremely desirable, and it's been a long time since I've … been with a woman."

"Mac."

He cut her off with a finger to her lips. "Laken, I mean, a serious long time. I've never been one to go into relationships lightly, and my lifestyle hasn't been conducive to relationships."

Laken felt her heart jump at what he revealed. She'd sensed Mac wasn't the sleep around type, but he was saying it was more. He would have to be in love with a woman to sleep with her, and there hadn't been many.

"Mac, I've never slept with a man. I plan on waiting until my wedding night."

A smile spread across his lips. It burned in his eyes and caught her breath. His hands came up to frame her face while his lips descended.

"You don't mind?" She gasped out when they came up for air.

"Not in the least."

"A lot of guys think I'm a prude or just plain strange."

"I'm not most guys."

"No, you're not." The feeling behind the words swelled in her. "Mac, I know it's only been a couple days, but I think I'm falling in love with you. Is that going to scare you away?"

"I think I started falling in love with you the moment I saw you looking so lost at the police station. Even when I thought you were nuts, I was still drawn to you for some odd reason that wasn't at all sexual. Well, maybe a little – you're beautiful," he teased, stroking her cheek. He eyes drift over her as a serious look spread over his face. "But there is something special about you."

Too nervous to go into the last sentence, Laken honed in on the previous one. "Nuts. Thanks."

"You're welcome." He let a little laugh out.

"I didn't sleep well last night because it hurt to think you–"

He cut her off again with a finger to her lips. "I was miserable too. I never want to hurt you again." He pulled her up to capture her lips.

Laken surrendered herself over to his kiss, returning it with pleasure.

A growl ripped from his throat and he broke off holding her close. "We have to stop this now. You need to get some rest. I better go."

Laken missed the feel of his body the moment he

moved away. It was as if part of her had been taken from her. He turned to look back at her and swooped in. The kiss was hard and stole her breath, then he was gone.

"Lock up after me and right to bed," he ordered, heading for the door, grabbing his jacket from the hall tree as he passed.

Laken could only stare after him, hugging her knees to her chest. Mac hadn't said when she'd hear from him again, but there was no doubt that she would. He'd told her he was falling in love with her. Happily, she did as he ordered. Sleep came almost immediately when she closed her eyes, and a short while later − the dream.

Chapter Seven

The Hunter's stride was purposeful, smooth, taking Laken along with him. She could see the woman in front of them. She wanted to yell to the woman to run, but The Hunter's thoughts answered back.

There was no need to hurry. The stupid woman can't get away. So absorbed in her own world, thinking how she had come out on top, she didn't even realize he was there.

He heard her boasting about her new job, and she didn't need some jerk hitting on her. How she told the man to get lost. Who did she think she was to treat her betters like that? She was just another back-stabbing witch. But, he was more powerful than her.

Fire burned in his veins.

The distance between him and the prey diminished. He could taste the thrill of the kill now. Laken sensed it, and it made her stomach roll. She fought to pull back, but she was trapped. The clicking of heels on the sidewalk thundered over the soft whispers of The Hunter's shoes.

Exhilaration leapt inside him when he saw the alley. *It was perfect. The street was empty, no one to see her go in and not come out.*

"No." Laken tried to scream, but nothing came out as he rushed forward.

At the last second the woman must have realized he was there because she turned. Her cry was hardly a squeak. She stumbled back into the alley, turned and ran. Laken cheered her on until she got a taste of the satisfaction in

The Hunter for the prey being herded just where he wanted her. He swooped in after her.

Laken's heart pounded with his, and she tried to fight, clawing at him from the inside, but his excitement rose higher. Adrenaline, driven by the anticipated kill, flared through him. He burned with madness.

His hand came out to catch the back of the woman's collar. The yank dropped her to her knees. She cried out like a frightened animal. He gloried in it.

Dragging her back to her feet, he turned her to face him. As she came around, her hand shot up, arching toward his face. Laken caught a glimpse of something in her hand at the same time as The Hunter did. His hand knocked hers aside just as the spray burst out. It missed The Hunter's face but was close enough to bring water to his eyes, blurring Laken's vision.

Through watery waves she saw The Hunter's hand strike the woman across her face. "Stupid witch." The words roared in her mind. Before the woman could muster another attack, he pulled her back to him, slamming her hard against his body.

Fear filled the woman's eyes as she looked up into his face. Laken knew his hand was rising up. She screamed again in her mind, but it did nothing to stop the knife from plunging down. Shock registered on the woman's face a second before emptiness filled her eyes.

He released her giving a little shove so that she fell face down amidst the trash. Her arm banged off a garbage can, but The Hunter didn't seem to notice. He stepped forward and bent down, deliberately wiping the knife off on her, leaving a garish red streak.

Straightening, he deliberately placed his foot in the small of her back and ground it down before turning away. The calmness that came over him allowed Laken to slip free.

CB80

Laken awoke sweat-soaked and shaking. Her head and heart pounded. Images of the dream flashed before her. It took three tries for her trembling fingers to lock onto the quilt to pull it up over her body.

Several minutes elapsed before the tremors eased enough that she decided she could try for the lamp beside her bed. She managed to click it on just as she knocked it over. Fortunately, it didn't break or go out. The warm glow it gave off helped push back the lingering shadows of the dream, but there was only one thing that she could think of that would help rid her of the fear.

It wasn't until she picked up her cell phone from the night stand that she realized she didn't have Mac's number. Despair swamped her as she stared at the phone for a full minute before her brain came up with the realization that he'd tried to call her several times and that his number would be recorded in recent calls.

The relief of seeing it there brought tears to her eyes, and she pressed the dial. With each ring she feared he wouldn't answer then a groggy voice came over the phone.

"Yeah."

For the first time Laken glanced at the clock and realized it was after one o'clock. "Sorry." The word trembled out. She shouldn't have called, but it was too late now, and she needed to hear his voice desperately.

"Laken." Her name came back over the line, now sounding totally alert. "What is it?"

"I dreamed," she got out, pushing back the sob before it could slip out.

"I'm sorry," his voice was soothing. "I guess it was too much today having you go over it like that. We can sit and talk until you feel all right."

"No," she gasped out, stopping him. "He killed again. It wasn't the same. He killed again." This time the tears made it free with the cry in the phone.

There was silence on the line a second before he said,

"I'll be right there, stay on the line with me."

Laken could hear movements from the other end. She thought about telling him not to come but couldn't bring herself to do it. Cuddling into the blanket, she listened to him ramble to her about nonsensical things. His voice pushed way the chill from her body.

It was only fifteen minutes later that he told her he was coming up the stairs, and she crawled from the bed, pulling the blanket with her. She staggered the first steps, unsteady on her feet as she made her way to the door. The instant she got the door opened, he caught her to him, which was a good thing because her knees gave out.

Mac felt her sag against him and tightened his hold. The shivers that shook her body were alarming, as was the slight temperature he felt lingering on her forehead. Shifting slightly, he lifted her into his arms, using his elbow to close the door.

"You shouldn't carry me," she mumbled against his neck.

"We're not going far. My leg can make it." Placing weight on it cautiously, he prayed that it was true. It wouldn't look real macho if he fell.

It was with relief he settled on the couch with her cradled across his lap. He relished the feel of her arms wrapped around him. She clung to him as he moved his hands over her back. He forced himself to be patient until she was ready to tell him what happened.

He wondered if she'd fallen asleep just before she finally raised her head to look up at him. "I'm sorry I woke you, but thank you for coming."

"You're welcome." He kissed her forehead, pleased to feel her temperature seemed back to normal. "You want to tell me about it?"

"No," she said honestly, "but I will." She took him through the vision step by step.

"Did you know the victim?" he asked when she

finished.

She shook her head. "No. I've never seen her before."

"Do you know where it was?"

"No, it wasn't anywhere I could recognize."

"Okay, I want you to think of him, anything that you can recall. All impressions you got."

Laken sat quiet a minute, a shudder shook her body. "I think he was at a club or a party. There was something about someone trying to pick her up, and she rejecting him. That was what drew The Hunter's attention."

"Good. You always refer to him as The Hunter. Why?"

Laken looked shocked as if she didn't realize it. "I don't know. I guess it's because that's how he sees himself. He doesn't think of himself as a killer. He thinks they deserve to die. That they've forgotten their place, and he's to hunt them down and exterminate them."

She paused, thoughtful, then continued. "It's that they think they're as good as men. That's why he kills them. He's proving he is better than they are." Shivers went through her again.

Mac tightened his hold, and she rested weakly against him. "It's okay." He pressed a kiss to the top of her head. "It's okay," he repeated. "Sweetheart, do you think you can describe her to me?"

Laken's nod was slow in coming. "She's taller than me and wearing a business suit with slacks. Her hair was dark. Brown, I think. It hung straight at her chin. Her eyes were dark too. I'd guess they were also brown. She was pretty with sharp features. You know what they call a chiseled nose, strong chin. She had an assertive air about her, strong-willed."

Yes. The fight back with pepper spray would fit, Mac thought. "Anything else you can give me?"

"No, I don't think so."

He pulled the blanket still wrapped around her up higher and continued to rub his hands over her back. She relaxed in his arms. After a while, he felt her lips press down over his heart and smiled, warmed by the motion. "Feeling better?"

"Yes."

"Ready to try to get some sleep?"

She was quiet a moment as if she really had to debate about it. "I think so," she finally answered.

"All right, let's get you to bed." He eased her off his lap so he could stand then helped her up.

When he started to lead her to the bedroom, she hesitated. "I need to lock up after you."

"I'm not leaving. I'll be out here on the couch if you need me." He pressed a kiss to her forehead before drawing her toward the bedroom. The first thing he saw was the lamp on the floor. With a questioning glance, he leaned over to pick it up.

"I knocked it over when I tried to turn it on. I should have picked it up before going to the door."

"No harm done. Do you have a blanket I can use?" he asked as she climbed into bed.

"The top of the closet. There are several."

He pulled up the fuzzy blanket and the old-fashioned quilt, and spread them over her before placing a quick kiss on her lips. "Get some sleep. I'm right here."

He had to force himself to turn away from the appealing sight she made in the bed. Opening the closet, he took down two blankets. He made it to the doorway before he gave in to the urge to look back.

She was settled in bed, her eyes half closed with sleep. A smile crested her lips as she watched him. His heart pounded. He longed to go to her. "Good night." He forced the words out, shoving his hands into his pockets to keep from reaching for her.

"Good night, Mac."

The soft reply ripped at him. Mac figured he wouldn't be getting much sleep, but after writing down her statement, to his surprise, he went right out when he laid down.

He woke to the smell of something cooking. When he shifted his head toward the kitchen, he was rewarded with the sight of Laken by the stove. She'd obviously showered and was dressed for work but still wore her slippers.

Light slipped in from the small window, framing her. She was so beautiful. When she turned and saw him awake, she smiled and his heart lurched. He wanted to wake up to that smile the rest of his life.

"Good morning." His voice rumbled sleep-roughened.

"Good morning."

"I didn't expect breakfast in bed."

"You're not in bed. And, it's the least I can do after last night. I hope you like omelets. It's what I had the ingredients for."

"Sounds great to me." Burnt toast would've been fine if he got to look at her while he ate it. "How are you feeling today?"

"Actually, better than I figured. Now what? Do I have to come make a statement?" she asked, putting the omelets on the plate.

"No. I don't have a crime yet. I wrote down everything after you went to bed last night so we'll go with that, but if you think of anything else, let me know."

"Mac, what if there was a murder?"

He got up, and came to stand behind her, and slid his arms around her, pulling her back against him. "Then we face it."

"I wish it would end." She turned, wrapping her arms around him. "But, I'm really glad you're here."

"Me too." He tilted her face up to kiss her. For a moment, everything was right with their worlds.

∞

"Mac, what is this? She's playing you. You're smarter than this." Jonesy tossed the notes Mac had made from what Laken had told him back on his desk. "She's figured out just how to get to you. You're the hero type. She calls you in the middle of the night and you come running to the rescue. She has you wrapped around her finger."

"I'm not asking you to help me." Mac glared up at him.

"No, but you're wasting time with this nonsense."

"I don't think it is nonsense. I think there really is something to what she dreams."

His partner snorted.

"Dr. Shannon believes her also, and I doubt she would be fooled by Laken's feminine wiles like you seem to think I am."

"You said Dr. Shannon was fascinated by the whole thing that happened during the hypnosis. Maybe it was all an act, a very convincing act. And you yourself were saying just last week how long it had been since you were in a relationship. You're vulnerable."

Mac couldn't keep in the roar of laughter. "I can't believe you said that. Where'd you get that from, Connie?"

This time the man looked decisively embarrassed. "We were talking. She's worried about you, too."

"She hasn't even met Laken yet. What did you tell her?"

"Just everything that happened and you can't say it wasn't weird."

"Okay, I can grant that. It was odd. But, you need to get a chance to get to know her. Laken is not like what you think." The doubt was still evident on Jonesy's face. "How about we all go for dinner? I'll call and see if she's free tonight. Is that good for you?" Mac knew he was challenging his partner and he'd accept it, so he was already reaching for the phone by the time the answer came.

"Yeah, we don't have any plans."

"Good," Mac waited as the phone rang.

"Hello." The greeting sounded distracted.

"Did I catch you at a bad time?" Mac asked her.

"Mac," Laken's tone warmed. "No. I'm just searching for a missing blueprint page I was assigned to redo today." There was the sound of shuffling in the background. "Robert's wife went into labor so he won't be in. He called and told me he did it, it's just not where it's supposed to be."

"Sounds like you need a detective."

"Only if you're volunteering."

"Actually, what I'm volunteering is dinner." He pictured her in his mind. The phone pressed to her ear as she thumbed through papers.

"I think I still owe you one."

"Well, this dinner is with my partner and his wife." The noise on the line stopped. He couldn't even hear her breathing. "I want him to get to know you. I've talked him into giving you a chance."

"This is important to you?" There was no mistaking the hesitation.

"Yes, it is."

A sigh came over the phone before she answered. "All right, what time?"

Mac looked at his partner. "Seven, okay?"

Jones nodded, and Laken answered. "Okay." Her answer was followed by a gasp.

"Laken, you all right?"

"I can't believe it." There was definite distress. Her words sounded labored and he became alarmed.

"Laken."

"That dirty, rotten – He took my designs. He stole them. That's why I wasn't invited to the presentation, and he's been avoiding my questions."

"Laken, what is it?" Mac called her attention.

"What, oh, I told you about the presentation I was left out of, Hoster, my boss, he put his name on my plans for the Galaxy building. I just found a page from my design with the name plate changed, his name is on it. He took credit for my plans."

"Are you okay?"

"I don't know. Did he think I wouldn't find out? I can't believe it, after all that work." Pain filled her voice.

"I'll be right there."

"No, no, don't do that. It'll cause more trouble. He was ballistic when you were here before. He's looking for a reason to fire me. Now I know why. I'm going to see if I can talk to him. I'll see you tonight." The phone went dead in Mac's ear, and he found himself wanting to go to her, but held himself in.

Chapter Eight

Laken stared down at the familiar lines on the page. It was the third floor layout. Infuriated, she went on a search and came up with twenty-seven other pages that had Hoster's name on them. He hadn't even changed a single line. Anger filled her so tightly that it hurt to breathe. She fought to control the aggravation, but there was no holding back the need for answers. Out of habit, she rolled the pages up before heading in the direction of Hoster's office.

"Kathy." She moved past the secretary's desk. "I need to see Hoster."

"He asked not to be disturbed."

Laken didn't even slow a step.

Stewart Hoster looked up as she burst in. "What is this?" he demanded.

"That is what I'd like to know." Laken dropped the blueprint copies on his desk.

Hoster didn't even bother to look at them. "And," he said in simple arrogance.

"Those are my plans with your name on them."

"Wrong, they are company plans." He tilted his nose up.

"This is why you didn't let me present, because you were taking credit for my work." Laken fought to remain calm though she wanted to scream at him.

"I was doing what was best for the company. How would it look having a low level draftsman doing a project of this magnitude? What are you so upset about? If they are picked, you'll still get your bonus."

"But that was not what was promised, and you're taking the credit."

"What's the big deal? If they were my original plans, you would have done all the drawing up and making them fit with specs."

"But–"

"I suggest you'd better get back to work. You're already on probation."

"Probation?"

"Yes. And, if you want to speak to me in the future, make an appointment. I will let it go this one time, because it's obvious you're overwrought. I understand women can be moody."

Laken was about to object, but he cut her off before she could speak. "Now leave, Miss Williams, or you're fired." He looked back to the papers on his desk, totally dismissing her.

Stunned, Laken left the office.

Kathy was waiting outside the door and closed it behind her. "Are you all right?"

"He stole my designs and threatened to fire me." She shook her head trying to believe what had just happened.

"Yeah, calling him a slug is too nice a word for him."

"I can't believe he did that. Why would he?"

"Because he knows you're better than he can ever be. Better than any man in this office. You're brilliant and he's a blowhard riding on the backs of others. He plays the game really well, and you don't play it at all. What are you going to do?"

"I don't know, but I don't think I can continue working under him."

"You're not going to do anything drastic, like quitting, are you?" Kathy reached to take her hands.

Laken squeezed them in reassurance. "I won't do anything rash, but I'm going to think about it. I think I'm going to see if I can get an appointment to see Mr. Warner."

"You're going to the big boss? Do you think that's wise?"

Laken knew that the head of the firm intimidated Kathy, but Laken had always thought he was decently pleasant, though she hadn't had a lot of dealings with him. He did have a little good old boy attitude, but he'd hired her right out of college without any experience. Mind made up, she answered. "Yes, I'm going to call and set an appointment."

Back at her work area, Laken called up to Mr. Warner's secretary and took the first appointment available, unfortunately, it wasn't until Monday morning. She settled down and tried to focus on work though her heart was not truly in it. The feeling that this was not the place for her and that it was time to break out on her own became more prevalent with each passing hour.

CঊৎৎO

Laken decided that Mac really knew his restaurants. The steak place where they went was fabulous. The rolls where hot out of the oven and so good they made her forget how rough the day was, and her trepidation about being there. Once she relaxed, Laken started enjoying herself. Mac's partner's wife, Connie, was a vivacious dark-haired pixie of a woman. It didn't take long to like her.

Mac's partner took longer to accept, especially after the two rocky encounters and the feeling of skepticism he gave off. Though, she guessed she really could give him that. Because her story was still hard even for her to understand and she was living it. She was just glad that Mac had told her there weren't any murder victims that fit her last dream. So maybe that was all it was, just a nightmare that happened to fit one that happened.

Fun and relaxation really came into the evening when Jonesy and Mac started to regale her with weird and hilarious things that happened in their jobs. When they finished eating Connie spoke up that she needed to go freshen up and invited Laken to go with her. Laken took the cue and excused herself.

"I know that was hardly subtle," Connie started once they were in the restroom, "but I wanted a private moment to talk to you."

Laken felt unease creep in with each word and was shocked when she continued. "I wanted you to know, I like you, and I was prepared not to. After what Marcus told me, I was expecting a whack job. And I couldn't figure how Mac could fall for you, especially this fast. He's seen too much to be fooled easily. Now, I can see why he's fallen for you. You're good for him. You're good together. There's a connection. You love him."

Laken couldn't get her voice to answer so she just nodded. The petite woman wrapped her arms around her and then beamed up.

"I'm so glad. Don't worry about Marcus. He'll come around. In fact, he already has. He just has to have time to get over that first impression."

"You mean me as a nutcase?" Laken squeaked out.

"That's the one. Wow, that's something." Open astonishment showed in Connie's dark eyes.

"It's something I wish would just go away," Laken let out.

"I can understand that. Totally freaky."

"Very."

"Well, hang in there and, if you just need to talk, give me a call."

"Thanks, I might do that. No one else knows about it."

Connie gave her another hug. "Shall we rejoin the guys?"

"Yeah." Laken followed her out, feeling like she'd made a new friend.

A half hour later, Mac followed her inside her

apartment. Catching her hand, he led her to the couch. Drawing her down with him, he pulled her into his arms, giving her a short, hard kiss. "Well, you seemed to survive the inquisition. How do you feel?"

"Good. I like Connie a lot."

Mac nodded. "It's hard not to like Connie. She's one of those people that everyone likes. What about Marcus?"

"Actually…" She leaned back in his arms to meet his gaze. "I like him better than I thought I would. He still doesn't believe me, but I can't hold that against him because I'm still having trouble with what to think. I do like him though."

"He admitted that he might have been wrong about you. He doesn't think I'm so crazy now for 'succumbing to your influence'. You're not as flaky as he thought. Nor a liar." Mac ran his fingers under her hair to massage her neck. She liked the feel.

"So I'm just slightly delusional," she said sarcastically.

"Pretty much so." He laughed, hugging her tight.

She turned in his arms to kiss him. "How does it feel being with a crazy woman?"

"Good. Real good." He slid his hands up in her hair again to tilt her head so he could kiss her. One arm came down around her waist, holding her tight against him.

When they broke, they only parted a couple inches. His hand stroked through her hair, luxuriating in the feel of the silk strands through his fingers, and a female presence alongside him. "So you enjoyed yourself?"

"Yes, I did. I like your friends."

"Are you going to tell me what's bothering you then?" He touched a finger under her chin tilting it up to him. Mac wondered if she was going to deny it and was pleased when she didn't.

"When you were on the phone with me today, I found one of the blueprint sheets of the plans that I did for the big presentation. The one I didn't get to present. Well, it had my boss' name on the name plate that's in the bottom corner. It tells what the plans are for, who designed them, and which page of the set, so on."

Frustration burned in her eyes. "Anyway, I confronted my boss about it, and he just brushed me off. He said they were company plans and it wouldn't look good for a lower level draftsman doing the plans for a project of that importance."

"You mean, outdoing all the upper level people," Mac remarked and was rewarded with a large smile.

"Thank you."

"Just making a logical deduction."

"Yeah, well, he basically told me, that was how it was and live with it, or I'm fired."

"You're kidding."

"No."

"What are you going to do?" He brushed his knuckles along her cheek.

"What makes you think I'm going to do anything?"

He just looked at her, cocking one eyebrow up.

"You're a pretty good, detective."

"That's what they tell me."

She smiled and sighed. "I made an appointment with the firm's head, Mr. Warner. Unfortunately, it's not until next Monday morning. For some reason, I get the feeling he won't do much about it. It's just so frustrating, after what they promised, all the work that I put in on it, and then not to be recognized at all. It's not fair. Hoster promised I would still get the bonus for it, but I don't know if I have faith in that now, and it's beside the point. I wanted to be able to say, I did that."

"I'm sorry." His hand came up to cup her cheek.

Laken turned into it to kiss his palm. "Maybe it's for the best. I've been thinking of going out on my own."

"You mentioned that before."

"Well, maybe this is the push I need to do it. If I get

the bonus, it would help, though it's not much."

"You wanted to get out of the city."

She nodded.

"Any idea where?"

"Not really. I can't go home because my family is from a real small town, and it won't support me. I need to stay close enough to the city for the contacts, and so I'm no more than a couple hours away if I need to come in for meetings."

"You have thought about this."

"Yes."

"Well, can you maybe think about a location just north of here, say about an hour and a half north? It's a college town. Real nice place, I think you'd like it."

"Mac?" She looked up, startled by what he was hinting at.

"I just want you to start thinking about it. See how it works in your equations ..." he paused, "and in your heart. I know it's soon, we've only know each other a week. But, it's been quite a week and well, one thing I do know is, I care about you, in fact, I think I love you. I want the chance to see if it will work for the rest of our lives. I'm not trying to hurry it, but please think about it."

Her eyes ran over his face searching for answers he hoped she saw there. "It feels so right," she whispered breathlessly.

"Yes, it does." He drew her back to meet his lips. Laken slid into his embrace and the feeling of love filled the air as the intensity of the kiss grew. In unison they broke. Laken laid her head on his shoulder, and they both fought to catch their breath. They stayed that way for some time.

"I better get going. Sleep tight." He thought of her last night's sleep. "Are you going to be all right?"

"I'll be fine."

He held her tight a minute more before he released her

so they could stand. His hand caught hers, drawing her up with him. They clung together again, both hating to lose the contact. She moved with him to the door, his arm around her waist. "Dream of me," he said as he turned her to him for a final kiss.

"I'm sure hoping to."

"I don't think there's any doubt you'll fill my dreams. I have to work the late shift tomorrow. I promised one of the guys a couple weeks ago to trade with him. So how about I call you and we meet for lunch?"

"That would be wonderful."

"Good." He kissed her long and hard, wanting to hold the feeling with him on the way home. He knew it would never satisfy him until she was his forever.

Chapter Nine

Usually working Sunday afternoon shifts didn't bother Mac, but today he wished he could be with Laken instead, even though they'd had lunch together Friday, started Saturday with breakfast then spent the whole day until he finally got his home cooked dinner with her, which they made together. He even went over to her apartment again for breakfast that morning. They'd gone for a walk in the park and then watched movies and talked until it was time for him to go to work. It had been a great weekend.

He glanced at the clock, three hours to go. Unfortunately, it would be too late to see Laken on his way home. Oh well, he'd see her tomorrow.

His phone rang, and a second later he headed out the door. At the entrance to the alley, he felt a sense of dread. Mac could see the crime scene guys unloading their gear. A tow truck stood halfway down the alley. An officer stood to the side talking to a man Mac figured was the driver. He headed toward them.

"Detective," the officer greeted him. "This is Mr. Erickson. He runs the tow truck. He found the body."

"Thanks." Mac turned his attention to the man who was in his late fifties, with a day's growth of whiskers on his face, tired eyes, and a paunch hanging over his belt. "Evening sir. Thank you for waiting to talk to me. Can you tell me how you happened to find the body?"

The man paled further and cleared his throat. "Got a call for an impound. It'd been setting here for a couple days, and the building owner there got tired of it because it's half blocking the dumpster and the garbage picks up tomorrow. When I got here, I checked the plates. It was listed stolen a couple days ago. So I walked around to check it out, that's when I saw her. She's kind of hidden back there. Looks like someone hit her then panicked and ran.

Mac asked a couple more questions and got his name then headed for the crime scene guys.

"Hey, Rob, another late night?"

"Only way I get to hang out with Amy," the tech replied, looking back at him.

Mac noticed the petite woman by the front of the car.

Amy spoke before he could greet her. "What can I say, dead people and night, just my thing."

"Ain't it every ones?" Mac grinned back. "So we got a hit-n-run?"

"Nope. You're going to want to walk around here and see this," Rob took up the conversation.

Mac didn't like the feeling the words brought and moved around the edge of the car to get a look at the body. The woman lay, face down, her head to the side. She would've been pretty if she hadn't been sitting out in an alley dead for what he guessed was at least a couple days.

His eyes locked on a small bloodstain on her back and the clearly evident grimy footprint ground just below it. The superlative slipped out under his breath.

"Yeah," Rob agreed. "There's no doubt about it. No rain to wash down the markings. That's why I asked that they call you. I'd make a real good guess that it's the same man."

Mac nodded. "You guys know the drill. I want everything you can give me as soon as possible. Especially time of death." Though he figured he already had that if he went with Laken's nightmare. He stared down at the woman who fit Laken's description down to her sharp features.

The night just got a lot longer and far more complicated for him.

Mac's leg had long passed aching by the time he made it home. Again the thought of pain meds the doctors had prescribed beckoned to him, but he refused to give into it. He swallowed down some ibuprofen before stretching out on his bed.

He hated the thought of having to tell Laken they had a body after all. She'd just started to relax. Feeling that maybe it was just a dream, and she wasn't having visions of murder. With everything she was handling at work, she really didn't need this. Neither did their relationship.

One thing was for certain, he needed to catch this guy and soon, or he'd kill again. And not only would he fail to protect another woman, but he was afraid Laken would see it again, and that made it more personal. The only problem was they didn't have a clue yet who the guy was.

∞

Laken felt a wave of nervousness sweep over her as she stepped into Mr. Warner's office. She'd woken early and spent the extra time trying to figure out what she was going to say and still had no idea. Taking a deep breath, she tried to force her legs not to shake.

"Miss Williams." Malcolm Warner looked over his desk. He was a big man, with a forceful manner that she found slightly intimidating. Still, she reminded herself, he had given her a chance right out of college. "You wanted to speak to me."

"Yes, sir." She followed the motion made by his hand and settled in one of the over-sized leather chairs in front of his desk. She wondered for a moment if the chairs were designed to make a person feel small, less significant.

"What can I do for you?" he asked when she hesitated trying to form her thoughts.

"I have a concern." She swallowed, to clear her throat.

This shouldn't be so hard. She was a professional, and she was in the right, though she felt like a child tattle-telling. "It's about the Galaxy proposal. It was open for all to put in a design."

"Yes. I'm aware of that. It was my idea."

"I worked up a set of plans, and they were chosen for final selection."

"Congratulations, I knew you were talented." There was almost something condescending in the cadence of the man's voice.

"The thing is, I did not get to be at the presentation with Mr. Sherman because I was told the wrong time on purpose. Mr. Hoster presented my plans under his name, going so far as to reprint them with his name plate."

She stopped talking, waiting for Mr. Warner's reaction. She was shocked when it came.

"And?"

"He took my plans."

"Wrong. He took company plans. You work for the company, and the plans were done for the company. Hoster did what was best for the company."

She was stunned by his words. "How can you say that?"

"Miss Williams, you are a junior member of the staff. Surely you can see that Mr. Hoster was correct in his action. You should be grateful. I assure you, you would not have been comfortable in the meeting. You should feel happy that he saw the possibility of the plans and decided to put his name on them so they would get considered."

Outrage started to build within her. "You're not serious." She leaned forward. "I spent two months, working nights and weekends on those plans, because I wanted to show I could do more than clean up and detail others' work."

"And you did quite a good job, but we must look at what is best for the company. What would you like me to do? Go to Mr. Sherman and tell him that the plans were made by a lowly draftsman, or I should say, woman. Think what it would do to the reputation of this company. There are several other contracts with the company riding on this if he likes the finished project. But, I will tell you what I'll do. It was promised a twenty-five hundred dollar bonus. I will double that to five thousand."

"He chose my plans," she gasped, letting out a breath. Knowing it was certain.

"That is enough Miss Williams. You need to get back to work. Mr. Sherman will be here soon. And I want to go over everything to be certain all is in readiness. Please, leave now. I don't want to hear any more about this. I will call and see the bonus is sent out immediately. It will be in your account today."

Like Hoster had, the man looked back down at the papers on his desk, totally dismissing her. Laken opened and closed her mouth trying to form an objection, but nothing would come. Giving up, she rose and walked out of the office, aware she had just been paid off. She also knew now, the decision about staying with the company was made – she was leaving.

She had nothing there, certainly no respect. It hit Laken what her role in the company was, and she wondered why she never saw it before. She was the token female. The only female that worked there that was not a secretary. She was the company's 'quota' because it wouldn't look good if he didn't hire any women. It didn't matter how good or talented she was. She was never going anywhere if she stayed.

Laken was so stunned her legs almost gave out on her. She'd thought that kind of bigotry was gone. She never even considered it. That's why she never saw it. She was raised to respect who you were, not your race or gender.

Looking back, she realized it should've been obvious. What she thought was because she wasn't one of Hoster's golfing buddies was, in truth, the nature of the firm.

By the time she reached her work station her decisions were all made. She sat down at her desk to write her resignation. When she finished, she was surprised there was no sorrow in leaving.

The only thing she was sorry about was not getting to see her plans come to fruition. There would be nothing stopping her from going to see the building when it was finished, and though no one else would know she'd designed the building, she would.

That thought brought another. When had Hoster copied the plans? She had made a few final changes the last week and hadn't run them until the night before. Had Hoster gotten the final corrected plans out of her work area, or had he used the earlier ones from the copy room.

Drawn by the need to know, she made her way down the hall to where the large machine that could do blueprints was located and the plans stored. It didn't take long to find the plans.

For a minute, she felt the wave of satisfaction that Hoster hadn't pulled the finished plans. Then she thought of her building – the Galaxy Building. Mr. Sherman didn't deserve the problems caused by changes in the plans. It wasn't his fault what her bosses were doing to her. He deserved the best she could do, and she wanted it to be perfect because it was hers, whether anyone else knew it.

A spear of righteous indignation shot through her. Laken hurried back to her work area and drew out the finalized copy of the plans. She stared at them a second, then, mind made up, hurried upstairs bypassing Hoster's office to Mr. Warner's. The young secretary looked up as she strode toward her.

"I need to see Mr. Warner for a second."

"He's not available," the woman answered curtly.

"It will only take a second."

"He just left for lunch with Mr. Sherman," she said as

if Laken should've known and was late getting there. Fat chance she would have been invited.

"Here, put this on his desk." Laken dropped the resignation on the secretary's desk before hurrying for the elevator. Her ire rose with each floor she went down. She ran from the building but didn't even have to search for the men. They were right in front of her, waiting for the car to be brought around to pick them up.

Driven now, Laken stepped forward. "Mr. Warner."

Hoster moved to cut her off. "What do you think you're doing?" He hissed at her.

Laken shifted around him at the last moment and thrust the roll of plans out in front of her. "Here," she said forcefully. "When Hoster took my plans, he didn't take the finished set. I had added a few pertinent changes to make them better. And, though I think what you did was unethical, they are still my designs, and I want them to be perfect. If the builder goes by the other pages some problems may arise."

"Miss Williams." There was no missing the threat in Warner's voice, but she ignored it.

"Mr. Sherman does not deserve the problems. He is paying for the best and deserves the best. These are the best."

"You're fired," the man growled out obviously forgetting they were standing on the busy street with a client.

"You can't fire me. I quit. My resignation is already on your secretary's desk. I wouldn't work for someone who does things like you do." Fury radiated through her. "And I'd better get the bonus that was promised me, or I will bring charges." She turned away, back straight, heading back for the building.

Laken had just reached for the door when a hand extended over her shoulder and pressed on the glass in front of her, halting her action. Laken spun ready to meet the coming attack then froze.

"Young lady." The voice was unfamiliar, but the tall man with graying temples, dressed in a suit that cost more than what she made in a month, was not. "Let me understand this, it was you who designed my building?" Mr. Sherman asked directly.

Laken swallowed hard. Now that the indignation had burned off, she felt shaky and self-conscious. She swallowed back the tears that threatened to clog her throat. "Yes, sir. I did."

"I liked the plans immensely." He handed her a card. "Call me. I have several other buildings planned for in the near future. I'd like to discuss them with you."

Laken wasn't sure what to say, so extended her hand. "Thank you, sir. My name is Laken Williams."

"Laken, unusual name, I'll remember it. Thank you for the excellent work." He shook her hand and walked off.

Laken could only stare after the man, stunned. Her frustration slipped into amazement. Her eyes dropped to the card he'd handed her. It was his personal card. He had just handed her − her future.

If she did just one building for him, it could set her career. And she didn't have to feel guilty for stealing it away because she knew they'd only been contracted for the one building, hoping to pick up others. It had been their decision to be underhanded. Also, she had never had to sign a clause promising not taking a client for a particular length of time after she quit. Probably because they never saw her as a threat.

Her excitement flared. She really did have a chance to make it on her own. She turned to push open the door when the chill of dread hit her like a sledge hammer to her back, almost taking her to her knees. Her breath caught, and her body trembled with cold as heat burned across her forehead.

She clung to the door frame oblivious to all around her.

It wasn't until someone bumped into her and pushed her through the opening that the feeling passed. Slowly, her body started to return to normal, but the sense of unease remained.

Laken steadied herself and turned back to look through the tinted glass. People crowded the area outside, some standing and talking to others, most hurried by on the sidewalk, the average scene of people coming and going. But out there – something was wrong. No, not something – someone.

She studied the people trying to see who might be a killer, because if she wasn't wrong, he was out there. He was watching – her.

ဆဲ်ဆ

He watched her stride to the door, the back stabbing witch. He'd seen it all, the way she challenged the men. She gloated that she was better than them. That she was the best. Made the men look like the wrongdoers, and then putting a spell over the other man to get his notice, to steal away the business, to come out ahead. She was evil. She had to die.

He studied her, bringing his finger to his mouth. Yes, there it was. He knew her. The taste of her. That was what had drawn him here. It was to see her. She had to die.

Chapter Ten

Laken was still trembling when she made it back to her work area. She wondered if she should call Mac. Of course that was foolish, she had no proof the man was out there or who he was. No, it had to be her imagination. Either that or she was going crazy, which was just great now that she had found a man she loved. Determined not to let the thought take hold, she settled in cleaning out personal items after managing to snag a couple of copy paper boxes.

She was almost finished when her phone rang. She scooped it up. "Hello."

"Hi," Mac's voice greeted her. "What's up?"

"What do you mean?" She turned her whole attention to the phone.

"You sound a little distracted."

"Yeah." She took a deep breath. "I'm packing up my stuff. I quit my job."

"What happened?" His concern reached across the line to her.

"Basically, Mr. Warner didn't see anything wrong with what Hoster did. He said it wouldn't look good for a lowly, female draftsman to be representing the company. He upped my bonus to drop it and get back in line."

"Which, I'm guessing you didn't. You okay?"

"Yes. Actually, I am."

"So tell me what you did." There was a knowing quality in his voice that made the whole situation feel better.

"I wrote my resignation, and then realized that Hoster had copied an old set of prints so I took the new ones to Warner and gave them to him right in front of Mr. Sherman, the client who the plans were for."

"Oh boy," Mac laughed. "I bet they loved that."

"Yeah, I still can't believe I did that. I mean, it was right down on the street. They were just leaving for lunch."

"You chased them down?"

"I wasn't thinking of that, I was just kind of upset."

"So what happened? I didn't get a call for a homicide, so I take it, it didn't turn violent."

"No, but he told me I was fired."

"Ouch," he said, drawing it out.

"Actually no. I told him I had already handed in my resignation."

"Nice."

"Then something incredible happened. Mr. Sherman caught me before I got back into the building and gave me his card. He wants me to call him about doing another building for him."

"You're kidding! That's great."

"Yes. I can't believe it. I'm without a job. I should be panicking, but I'm not. I'm excited."

"Well, good for you is all I can say. So how are you getting home? I'm guessing you took the bus."

"Yes."

"Okay, I'll come get you. Are you about ready?"

"Yes, but you don't need to."

"I know. I'll be there in ten minutes. Love you." The phone went dead, and Laken smiled happily.

As promised, Mac walked in ten minutes later. Her breath caught. He looked tired under his smile, and his limp was more pronounced, but there was nothing lacking in the kiss he gave her. She slipped her arms around him luxuriating in the feel of being in his arms. He was just what she needed to wipe away the last tendrils of unease from what she'd experienced earlier.

She settled back, raising her hand to caress his cheek. It was slightly prickly with stubble. "Rough night?" she asked gently.

"Long one," he murmured, nuzzling her neck

She sensed there was more to it than that, and he must have read her perception because he added. "I'll tell you about it later. I think I should take you to lunch to celebrate right now. You all ready?"

"Yes."

He picked up the bigger of the two boxes, letting her take the smaller. "I'll follow you."

Laken stopped to say good-bye to Kathy. The secretary was shocked by the news, but most of her surprise seemed to be focused on Mac. They'd just started for the elevator when Kathy caught her arm and held her back.

"Laken," she whispered conspiratorially, "That man is − wow."

Laken could only laugh. "Yeah." She smiled. "I think I'm going to have to marry him. See you later." She hurried to catch up to Mac.

"Call me in a few days." Kathy's voice followed her, but Laken lost the thread of the thought when she met Mac's eyes. They bore down into her, making her insides jump.

"Did you mean that?"

She didn't try to play innocent. "You heard?"

"Oh, yeah. I have extremely good hearing."

"I'll have to remember that." Her heart thundered in her chest, and she wondered if he could hear it. "Yes."

"Yes," he repeated, the intensity deepened in his eyes.

"Well, there's still a lot of things to face first, and we haven't known each other long, and ...." Luckily, the elevator arrived saving her from coming up with something else to say.

She stepped inside. Mac followed her in, put his box

down on the floor and took her box, setting it on the other. Then, ignoring the other two people in the elevator, he pulled her into his arms. His mouth came down capturing hers. It took only a second for her to become lost in the kiss that was full of promise and passion.

It wasn't until a throat cleared loudly that they broke to the sight of a crowd waiting to get on the elevator at the ground floor. If the elevator had stopped on the way down for more people, Laken sure didn't notice.

Mac gave a crooked grin, handed her the top box, calmly picked up his box, and led the way out with a cocky, "good day", to the people waiting.

Laken was still blushing when they reached his car. "I can't believe I just did that. I was making out in an elevator," she said, mortified.

He just laughed. "Lady, I'd say you just made one grand exit. And I, for one, found it very enjoyable."

She looked up at him, shook her head and joined him in laughter.

Laken wasn't laughing an hour later, after they finished lunch and were back at her apartment, when Mac finally got around to telling her about the new body. She sat silently on her couch as Mac settled beside her, with a comforting arm around her shoulder.

"She's real," Laken whispered out through tears. "I really wanted to believe that it was all just a dream."

"I know, sweetheart. I'm sorry. I wish I could have waited longer to tell you, but I need to go over what you told me again in case you might have remembered anything more."

Laken nodded and started to go back over everything she remembered while Mac took notes. He probed for all the details he could then held her to him. She really hadn't added much from the first time, but had clarified several points from his notes.

After a while, he cupped her face and tilted her chin up

to him. "I have to go write this up," he said gently. "How about, when I come back, I make you dinner, and we settle on the couch and watch movies all night."

She managed a weak smile. "Yes."

She sat there after he left, wondering what he could see in her, other than she was psycho.

A couple hours later, Mac came down the hallway toward Laken's apartment with a grocery sack in one hand and whistling to himself. Despite Laken's nightmares and the murder case, life was good again. He had a beautiful woman waiting to be impressed with his culinary talents, and a couple of funny old movies sure to lift the spirits while they cuddled together on the couch. It sounded like the makings of a wonderful evening to him.

He'd just reached her apartment when the door across the hall opened. Instead of the orange-haired old woman, a man stepped out. He would've been in his mid-to-late thirties, descent looking, average build. When he saw Mac, he gave a derisive smile and spoke.

"If I was you, I'd just leave now. Take it from me, pretty packaging, but she ain't giving any."

Mac cocked his eyebrow but kept his expression blank. "What's that?"

The man nodded his head to Laken's apartment. "Take it from experience, she's one of those prim, too good for any man type. A real stick in the ass, ice queen."

"Really, I found her fun, intelligent, and warm."

Laken picked that moment to open the door. Mac stepped forward, wrapping his free arm around her, hauling her up against him and kissing her with enough heat to raise the temperature in the hall. Before he closed the door, he glanced back over his shoulder, giving the man a totally predatory look that said she was his.

"I think I'm going to start listening so I can greet you more often if you're going to kiss me like that." Laken fanned her face.

He turned his attention to her with a devilish grin. "Just staking my claim, I hope that doesn't bother you."

"Not at all." She wrapped her arms around his neck to stake one of her own.

ဆာ

The next afternoon, Mac's doctor appointment went pretty much how he figured it would. Continued physical therapy twice a week, but the prognosis for much more improvement wasn't great. Though he figured he was quite fortunate, he could've lost the leg from the knee down, or he could've been forced to use a cane or a brace the rest of his life.

As it was, his limp wasn't too pronounced, except when he was tired or tried to run. He didn't like it when the doctor warned him he might be facing another surgery in the future to remove scar tissue from the joint. Still, he'd face that when it came.

Jonesy looked up at him when he approached his desk, a frown furrowed the man's face. "What'd the doc say?"

"About the same. It's healing well. See you in another month. He'll send his actual report to the review board at the end of the week with the physical therapist's comments." When his partner just nodded, Mac studied him closer. "No comments that it's going to be no big deal, or are you finally accepting the inevitable, too."

Jonesy shook his head. "It's not that. Mac, the captain sent Pearson and Timothy to bring Laken in for questioning."

"Questioning. You mean to arrest her! For what?" Fury burst from him.

"Not arrest her. Just detain her. She knows too much about the murders. Things that we never released. Things only the murderer could know. I tried to talk him out of it. I urged him to let me call and ask her to come down or even wait for you. He wouldn't listen." Jonesy looked up with sympathy in his eyes.

ALYSIA S. KNIGHT

"They left already?"

"About twenty minutes ago."

"You should've called me." Mac was already heading for the elevator.

"I didn't know when you'd be done. Mac, don't do something stupid."

The comment fell on deaf ears, and the closing of the elevator doors.

ᘒᘒ

Laken was just getting to the good part in the book when a knock sounded on the door. She raised her head and frowned at it a second before putting her book down with a sigh. She really didn't want to be disturbed. It was the first time she'd had time to sit down and read in the last couple months, and she had relished it. Never, she vowed, would she let her life get so controlled that she would miss out on the simple pleasures like she had.

She thought of Mac just before reaching the door. There was nothing simple about her greatest pleasure. Mac was a truckload of disturbances to her senses, and she was enjoying every one of them. Things were happening so fast between them, but already she couldn't imagine her life without him.

She looked through the peephole, and caught sight of two men in the hall, not recognizing either. She hesitated, checking the door bar before cracking the door open. "Yes?"

"Miss Laken Williams?"

"Yes." Nervousness settled in.

"I'm Detective Timothy and this is Detective Pearson."

With her thoughts already on Mac, her insides shot right to panic. "Mac, has something happened to him?" The words ripped from her with a wave of panic. "Just a minute." She shut the door to release the safety bar and pulled it all the way back open. "Is Mac all right?"

The two men looked at each other.

106

"You mean Detective MacDaniels?" the other detective asked.

Laken let out a sigh at the men's obvious confusion which meant they weren't there about Mac. "Yes, sorry. You wanted to talk to me about something else." She was too relieved to pick up the men's dour expressions for a moment then she looked from one to the other. "What's going on?"

"Miss Williams, we need to take you down to the station for some questioning."

The nervousness was back with a feeling of dread. "I don't understand, why didn't you just call? Why didn't Mac come?"

"We were assigned to handle this."

She took an instinctive step back when they moved toward her. "What is this?" Her breath caught in her lungs and became ragged. "I'd like to talk to Detective MacDaniels. I already gave him a statement."

"I'm afraid that's not possible. He's not at the station at the moment."

She glanced at the clock, stepping back again, feeling swamped with fear and the pain of betrayal. "His doctor appointment."

Neither man made any comment, but one reached behind his back and drew out a pair of handcuffs.

Laken couldn't keep back a squeak of protest. "You're arresting me? Does Mac know?"

"You are not under arrest as of yet, Miss Williams, but the cuffs are as a precaution. Please turn around and put your hands on the wall."

Pain yanked at her heart again as she followed directions. The hands that patted down over her sweater and old faded jeans were impersonal but still brought a sense of revulsion at being touched so.

"Please, tell me, does Detective MacDaniels know?" The words tore at her as she felt the metal bite down on her wrist. Her arm was brought down and then the other wrist was caught and fastened. Laken flinched this time from the pinch. The two men remained stoically silent as they drew her to the door.

"Wait a minute, my keys."

"Where are they?" The man, Pearson, who stood to the side, asked.

"In my purse, on the shelf in the closet." Laken managed to get out, before she was led through the door. She stood and waited while the door was locked.

With each step down the stairs, the pain in her dug deeper. Her surroundings faded away into a sea of uncertainty. This couldn't be happening to her. She was being arrested for murder. A murder she'd dreamed.

Where was Mac? Surely, he would be here if he knew. He loved her. He said he did, and she didn't doubt that, but where was he?

Her thoughts were so tied up she didn't realize they were outside until Pearson jerked her toward the open car door held by Timothy.

Fear slammed into. She stumbled. The Hunter, he was there. He was watching. Hunting. Panic flooded her. "Wait," Laken cried out and tried to turn, to see if she could find The Hunter.

The man holding her arm jerked her back around, sending pain ripping through her shoulder. Already unsteady, her foot barely caught the edge of the curb before it slipped off and she went down, twisting it painfully underneath her. Unbalanced by her hands behind her back, she had no way to catch herself.

The hand on her arm dug in, but it couldn't stop her head from clipping the doorframe. Pain and lights flashed through her head, joined by a stabbing pain in her leg as she hit the ground. Everything faded away for a second before she was able to lock on what sounded like Mac calling her name.

Chapter Eleven

Mac brought the car to a screeching halt in the middle of the street. The sight of Laken in handcuffs ripped at his heart. Forlorn was not nearly deep enough to describe the look about her. Then, in the time it took him to get out of the car, he saw her fall. His heart lurched. He ran toward her but had no way to stop her from hitting the ground, or her head clipping the side of the car as she went down.

"Laken!" he called her name. "What are you doing?" He glared the other detectives away and came down beside her. She whimpered as he pulled her into his arms. "I have you," he murmured, tilting her head up to see where she had bumped it.

"Mac." She seemed dazed by his presence.

"It's all right."

A small stream of blood trickled down the side of her cheek originating from just below her hairline. Mac wanted to swear but held it in, pulling a handkerchief from his pocket and pressing it over the cut. "Get these cuffs off her," he growled.

"We're to take her in," Pearson came back defiantly.

"And you're doing such a good job of it," he snapped.

"Stay out of it," Pearson barked back at his sarcasm. "You've already compromised things enough."

Mac sent him a fierce look at the comment. "I'll take her to the station." He started to fish out his own key.

"Mac, Captain sent us to bring her in because you're involved with her," Timothy put forth. "You need to back off and let us do it."

"She's not under arrest." Mac fought down the urge to scoop her up in his arms and run away with her. Not that his leg would allow him to do that. Just kneeling on the curb beside her had it on fire with pain. "At least, let me get these handcuffs off long enough to look at her."

Laken had been leaning against him, quiet. When he released her hands, they slid around him and she clung to him.

"It's all right," he whispered down. "Let me take a closer look."

Laken shifted back then cried out, releasing him to wrap her arms around her leg, drawing it up.

Mac saw the blood soaking the pant leg just below the knee. "Easy." He caught her hand, pulling it away. "Sit up here." He lifted her to the seat of the detective's car then started to ease up her pant leg. At her whimper of pain, he took out a pocket knife and sliced up the well-worn denims she wore.

This time the swear word almost slipped out. There was a gash a little over an inch long in her leg. A piece of glass from a broken bottle protruded from it. "Get me the first aid kit," he ordered, using his handkerchief once more to wipe away blood. "This is going to need stitches."

He looked up at Laken who still hadn't said anything since his name. "You okay?"

She nodded. "You came." Her voice was barely over a whisper.

"As soon as I found out. I didn't know anything about this. I promise. I was at my appointment."

She gave him a forced smile then flinched with pain.

"Don't worry, I'll get this taken care of," he reassured her. She looked so frightened. "We'll get you to the hospital, and they'll have it stitched up in no time. Slide on back in the seat and I'll ride with you."

He turned and tossed his keys to Pearson. "Follow us

in my car," he ordered, taking the first aid kit from Timothy. He slid in beside Laken surprised his command actually worked.

CRYO

He couldn't get to the witch. He felt the heat of frustration. First, that man had been around her. A cop. He was a cop. Anger speared through him. She was working her spell on the cop. He was protecting her. But she didn't have the others fooled, he thought with satisfaction, thinking of them bringing her out in handcuffs.

His mood soured immediately, though, he couldn't get to her, at least not yet. He just had to be patient. He would be the one to get rid of her. The knowledge burned in his stomach. It was his job to kill them. It was his right.

He needed to hunt.

CRYO

They had driven a couple blocks when he heard Timothy chuckle from behind the wheel. "Pearson's ticked at you. It's a good thing he's not driving your personal car. I think he'd be tempted to drive it into a wall."

"Well, I'm not too happy with him at the moment either. You guys didn't need to be so rough with her."

"She pulled back at getting in the car and fell."

"Yeah, when Pearson jerked her off the curb." Anger flared in Mac as his mind replayed the scene.

The hand that rested on his arm was soothing, as was the look Laken gave him when he turned his attention back to her. He wanted to slide his arms around her, but a glance at her blood on his hands kept them in place on her leg.

The smile she gave him was shaky. "I'm in trouble aren't I?"

"Nah, it's just a little cut, five or six stitches."

"I mean the murders."

He knew what she meant and sighed. "We'll work it out."

"They think I did it," she said with a straight

111

forwardness he had to respect.

"Don't worry, I'll get the guy and clear everything up."

She nodded. "I know, but I'm afraid he's hunting again." She looked like she was going to say something more and then stopped.

"What is it?"

She shook her head. "Nothing, just a feeling."

Mac knew that wasn't all but didn't get time to ask as they pulled into the hospital parking lot.

It was almost a two hour wait before the glass was taken out of Laken's leg and seven stitches put in. They gave her a tetanus shot. When they left the hospital, she also had a butterfly bandage on the cut on her forehead and an ice pack on her ankle, which was swollen from twisting it when she slipped off the curb.

At the station, she was taken into an interrogation room where she was grilled continually for several hours while Mac was forced to wait outside, unable to say anything, afraid they would make him leave. He knew he was on shaky ground at being pulled from the case because of his relationship with Laken, but didn't understand how they could not see that she was telling them the truth?

He wanted to go to her, to pull her out of the room. She looked pale and so weary. He wondered when the last time was that she ate. He watched Pearson slam his fist down on the table, making her jump. The man wore his anger well.

Laken tried to keep calm under it, but it was obvious it disturbed her. Mac was relieved when the man stormed out of the room.

ꝏ

The instant the door was closed, Laken's head dropped to her arms folded on the table. She wanted Mac, though she knew he wasn't allowed to come near her. She had heard it discussed when they brought her in and had seen Jonesy take his arm, drawing him firmly away. She hoped he didn't get in trouble. At the hospital, while waiting, he told her several times not to worry, but that was impossible.

She felt so awful. The pain pill they had given her at the hospital took away most of the throb from her head, leg and ankle, but they all still hurt, and the medication made her tired. What was worse, though, was the anxiety that hadn't left since she stepped out of her apartment building. She felt like ants were running up and down her neck and shoulders. She wanted to scream, but given where she was, she didn't think that was a very good idea.

She wished they would let Mac in to see her. She didn't doubt he was still there. He wouldn't leave her unless it was to hunt for The Hunter.

What was she going to do? When would they release her? She wondered if she should request a lawyer. They said she wasn't under arrest, but she couldn't leave. Pearson seemed to take great pleasure in telling her that they could hold her for forty-eight hours.

She must've dozed off because some time had passed when the door opened again. Her hopes for release plunged when it wasn't Mac. The female officer directed her down the hall. Fear filled her and she wondered this time if she was being arrested. The room she was taken to wasn't exactly a cell. It was small, barely the size of a walk-in closet. The only thing in it was a cot.

"Do you need the restroom?" the woman asked blandly.

Laken nodded.

"Behind there." The woman motioned to a spot where the wall jogged out. There was no door, only the wall giving her privacy.

A minute later, Laken forced herself to step into the little room, and the barred door was closed behind her. Okay, so maybe it was a cell. She'd never been claustrophobic but figured that this place could make her.

Still, it had a bed and that was all she wanted. Though, when she stretched out, sleep was slow in coming as her thoughts flip-flopped over everything that was happening. It was hard to really believe this could be true. She tried to be a good, honest person. And, she was in jail because she had a dream.

She finally slipped into sleep and the nightmare.

⊂ஐ∞

Laken could feel the anger in The Hunter. He wanted to kill. It had been denied him.

He scanned the bar. Laken knew the place. She'd been there before on a date. It was a popular spot with the young executive, go-getter set. It was too loud for her taste and seemed that everyone was competing with everyone else. The Hunter scanned the room and studied several women.

His focus stopped on two different women. He thought they deserved to die, but not tonight, they didn't fit what he wanted. His gaze stopped on another woman. She had the look, but she seemed properly submissive so he moved on.

Then he saw her. Her shoulder length, brown hair caught the light as she strode up to the bar. The skirt of her severely cut female suit was tight over her hips. Head held high. Set features proclaimed her to be dominant.

When a man moved into her space, she glared at him until he moved aside. She then put her nose up and looked away, dismissing him as if he were a fly. Drink in hand, she turned and surveyed the room, a tight smile on her lips, challenging any man to step forward, and she would cut them down.

Laken was trapped in the vision. Knowing what was coming, she fought to wake, to scream, but she couldn't get any sound out in the dream world or into the real one. The eager hatred of The Hunter ate at her. The anticipation of the kill became an inferno.

⊂ஐ∞

Mac wanted to punch something, but kept the anger down and fought for reason. "Why do we need to hold her? She hasn't done anything," he demanded, staring down at his captain. Amos Carter was a bull of a man. Though several inches shorter than him, Amos was built like an old heavyweight boxer. Mac had a lot of respect for the man, whose eyes glared out at him from his dark ebony skin.

"Then how does she know so much about the murders? You said you didn't give her any details." Amos looked at him, challenging him to say he did.

"No." Mac bit back his anger.

"I didn't think so. That woman knows too much, and I'm not buying the dream thing. That psychic stuff might be going hot in the world but not in my station."

"Why would she come forward if she was involved?"

"You know the answer to that. Some just like to challenge us to catch them. They can't resist waving the red flag under our noses. I want you to get your head on straight and find me some evidence, or you're off this case."

"Laken didn't do it. Dr. Shannon agrees with that."

The man hardly paused. "The doctor is going with her instincts. I'm going with facts, and the fact is, the woman knows things that only the killer could know. Are you going to throw away your career over her?" his captain challenged back.

"What career? We both know mine's over. It's only a matter of time until I'm forced to retire."

"You're better than any man on this force."

"Then why won't you trust me on this? She's innocent."

"That's your emotions talking."

"No, it's not. You say you want evidence, let's talk evidence. She isn't tall enough. For the angle of the knife entry, she'd need to be at least six feet."

"The woman's five-eight, put her in heels and that would put her close enough."

"Who would put on high heels to go killing people? Okay, scratch that. There are sickos that would, but the foot marks on the victims' backs were not made from a high heel. Do you think she stops and changes shoes? And does she look like she has the strength to hold a woman, approximately the same size as her, while she plunges a knife in her back?" Mac made another point, but before he got his answer, there was a knock on the door and an officer stuck his head in.

"Sorry to interrupt, but I was told to inform you immediately that there's a problem down in holding with your suspect."

"What suspect?" the captain barked, obviously annoyed by the interruption.

"Laken Williams. They said MacDaniels would want to know. I guess she's running a high fever. They've got a paramedic unit headed down there now."

Chapter Twelve

Mac pushed passed the officer, bursting from the room, not needing to hear more. He took the stairs at a hobbled gate, not waiting for the elevator. The three flights had never seemed so far. It was easy to find where Laken was by the people gathered around the opening.

"Let me through," he demanded, as he pushed his way past them. No one dared to question his right to enter the room. Two men from a paramedic unit were kneeling beside the cot, opening their cases. He recognized both men. They were good paramedics, but one look at Laken sent terror slashing into him. She lay still on the cot, her mouth partly open in a silent gasp. It looked like she was barely breathing.

"What's happening?" The words trembled as they came out of him.

"She's burning up. Possibly some kind of an infection. They said she cut her leg earlier." One of the men, Justin, answered, not looking up from settling an oxygen mask over her face and reaching for a blood pressure cuff. "It could be what she cut it on contained some kind of poison, or she's having a reaction to what they gave her at the hospital."

"Her temperature is a hundred and five point three," the other man, David, announced.

Justin looked up. "You certain?"

"Did it twice, we've got to bring it down." David was already reaching for cold packs in one of the boxes.

Mac's attention turned to the woman he feared he couldn't live without. Her stillness terrified him. "Laken." He moved past the men to place a hand on her head. Her skin branded him with heat as he ran his fingers along her forehead to stroke back her hair. It took all his force of will to remain calm and think.

His mind ran over what she said about the visions of murder and the fevers. He remembered the heat that was still on her skin the night of the last one and how it had raised during the hypnosis.

"Man, her pulse is going through the roof," Justin said.

"Temperature's one-o-five point four."

"Laken, come on, it's Mac. Listen to me. You've got to come back to me. Come on, sweetheart. I need you to listen to me. You can fight this. You're stronger than he is. Fight it."

She remained still.

"Laken!" He gripped her face between his hands. Mac felt lost, only able to look down at her and plead with his eyes, and then he saw a tiny intake of air raise her chest.

"Temp's a hundred and five even." The voice in the room declared.

"Come on, Laken. You can do it."

Her head jerked to one side and back. "No." The cry was barely discernible.

"No?" Justin glanced at him, but he focused his attention on her.

"Yes," Mac demanded. "Come to me."

Her head flipped back and forth again harder, as if she was struggling. She dislodged the mask. "No." she cried out again. It was filled with agony and fear. "He's ... going to ... kill her. He's hunting. Run!" The scream seemed to be ripped out, making everyone jump. "He's there. Run, run. Look back." She panted.

"Laken, you've got to fight him."

Her head now thrashed back and forth so hard that

Justin had to grab her to keep her from falling off the cot.

"Someone see if Dr. Shannon can get down here fast," Mac yelled over his shoulder. "Tell her it's Laken Williams. That she's locked in on the killer."

"Her temperature's dropped to almost hundred and four. Keep talking to her. It's working," David announced.

"That's it, Laken. Fight him." Mac stroked back her hair.

"He's going to kill. He wants to kill."

"Where is he? Can you tell me where? Something that you know, something that can help me stop him? Something that can save her?"

"Marinette," she gasped out.

"Marinette," he repeated. "The bar. Are they there now?"

Her head shook this time in a controlled shake.

"Can you see her?"

Laken cried out. "Look back. He's behind you. He can taste the kill. She deserves to die. It's his right to kill her. Thinks she's as good as a man. He saw the way she acted, looking down on men. She needs to be taught her place."

"Her temperature's climbing again."

"Laken, listen to me. Concentrate on my voice. Come on, you can do it. We can stop him, but you've got to help me."

"Dr. Shannon says she's on her way. She said you need to keep talking to her, do what you're doing. Try to get her to describe everything, and see if she can become detached from the killer," someone said behind him.

"Laken, I need you to tell me where he is. You can do it. Look around and tell me what you see."

A whimper tore deep in her throat.

Mac fought to push down the panic rising in him at her obvious pain. "You can do it. Come on, sweetheart."

"Street." The word finally managed to slip from her.

"Good, where? What can you see? Come on, read me a

sign."

"Bank."

"Good, what bank?"

"The Sip."

"Sip. Someone get units to Hawthorn and a hundred and sixth. Now!" Mac ordered, sending them to where a small coffee shop sat on the corner across from a bank. "Where are they Laken?"

She jerked up from the cot. "No, don't go, don't go … in. No, not."

"Temperature's spiking!"

Mac grabbed her shoulders tight, holding her still. "Laken, where at? Where is she going? Fight him, baby."

"Parking." The word barely made it out between gasps.

"That's it. Tell them to check the parking structure," Mac again ordered over his shoulder.

A whimper escaped her, tearing at him. "I have you. I'm here, but I need you to tell me where she is. Where are they, Laken?"

"Temperatures dropping again," David said again taking another reading.

"She's going up, she's walking faster. Needs to run … to get out of there. He's moving faster. The witch thinks she can get away. No!" Laken screamed. "Don't face him. Run. Run."

She jerked. Terror etched deep in her face. "Fight, fight him." The words struggled out of her as she stiffened on the cot, every muscle in her body going rigid. Her breath back to tiny pants. The paramedic pressed the oxygen mask back over her face.

The other paramedic swore. "Her vitals are spiking. Her body can't handle this."

"Give her something," someone yelled.

"We can't. She's not stabile enough."

"Laken," Mac yelled at her helplessly.

☙❧

Laken jerked. She saw the woman swing up her hand with her purse in it, but The Hunter knocked it away easily.

She was pathetic if she thought she could stop him. She was nothing compared to him.

He didn't see her other hand come up until the claws dug into his face. He roared in feral anger. Digging his fingers into her neck, he shook her roughly.

Did she think she could defy him?

Her head flipped back and forth. He pulled her up to face him, his hand going into his pocket to pull out the knife. He was raising it behind her back when her spit caught him in the face.

Another roar erupted from him as he drove the knife down. The woman went ridged in his hold, her scream failing as it came out. He let her drop. She landed on her side instead of face down. Angrily, he shoved her over with his foot, then placed it on her back, and ground down. But, it wasn't right. The calmness didn't come. She deserved to die. He didn't doubt that, but it wasn't right.

He stared down at her and raised his hand to wipe the spittle from his face. Displeasure instead of calm filled him.

It should've been the other one. That was what was wrong. It should have been the other. She was to blame. It was her fault. He ranted in his mind. He had to kill her before the hunting would be right again.

The sound of a car coming up the ramp filtered in just before The Hunter slipped into the shadows.

The police, it was the witch's fault. The last thought came just before she fell free, and Laken knew he was talking about her.

ೞ

Laken jerked again and went so limp Mac felt a new wave of panic. "Laken." Her name tore from him in a whisper. It was then he saw her chest draw in a deep breath. He felt a surge of hope, but inside, he wondered if that meant the woman, whoever Laken was seeing, was dead.

Well, he couldn't worry about that right now. It was someone else's job. His concern was the woman before him. Mac jerked as a hand came down on his shoulder. He hadn't seen Laura Shannon push her way into the room.

"It's okay, Mac, she's free now. Her body just needs rest."

"Temperature plunging. One-o-one point seven," the paramedic said as if confirming.

"Pulse is returning to more normal," Justin added to his partner.

"Laken," Mac whispered, and leaned forward to brush a kiss on her forehead. "It's okay. I'm here. Just rest now."

She sighed but didn't stir.

"She's stabilized," David announced, and a collective sigh came from the people crowded in the back of the cell and in the doorway.

"Keep monitoring her," the doctor told them. "You can transport her now. There shouldn't be any problem, though I haven't seen anything like that before.

"Shit, neither have I," Captain Amos Carter exclaimed loudly from the doorway. "Was that real?"

"Oh, yes," Dr. Shannon answered. "I hope you have men there."

"Yeah, we have it covered. Okay, everyone back to work. Show's over. Get her transported to the hospital to check her out." The captain's voice barked at the back of the crowd, but before anyone could move, a radio squawked through the already tense atmosphere.

Everyone froze, listening to the request for medic and ambulance at the parking garage. They found a victim with one stab wound to the back, but she was still alive. The already hushed cell picked up a tomblike stillness until they brought a gurney in and forced everyone out of the way.

Mac steadied her neck and shoulders as they shifted her to the gurney. Laken remained limp, her chest barely rising.

As the paramedic spread a blanket over her Dr. Shannon caught Mac's attention. "I'll stop by the hospital later. I'd like to put her back under if she's up to it. See if we can learn anything more, but I'd prefer to do it at the hospital in case we have troubles. What she goes through is very violent."

Mac nodded, "I'll be there with her," he stated the obvious and then started to follow the gurney out. At the doorway, Amos caught his arm pulling him back.

"I'm going to the hospital," Mac shot out, leaving no room for argument.

The captain nodded. "Figured. I still don't know what to think." The man's head shook in disbelief on his big thick neck. "Mac, they found the woman. She's still alive, barely. They aren't sure if she'll make it to the hospital, but if they hadn't reached her so soon…" The man who had seen a lot in his career looked down the hall after Laken in pure puzzlement. "I wouldn't have believed it if I hadn't seen it myself, and I'm still not sure I do." Amos removed his hand letting Mac go.

Mac understood what the man was saying. He'd believed her already, but still, what he'd just witnessed was enough to freak him out.

At the ambulance, Justin stopped him from getting in. "We don't need an officer. She isn't going anywhere."

"She's my fiancée." The lie came out so easy Mac decided it was close enough to the truth. It sure felt right.

"Your fiancée was in jail?" The man looked at him in disbelief.

"Long story, but she isn't under arrest. She witnessed a murder."

"I kind of feel like I did, too." The man let him pass.

They were almost at the hospital when Laken began to stir, but she settled under Mac's touch. Her eyes fluttered open as they lifted the gurney out.

"It's okay, sweetheart." Mac caught her hand that

didn't have the IV in, bringing it to his lips.

"He killed again." Her voice was rough and raspy, filled with pain that reflected in her eyes.

"Maybe not." He let out to give her a chance of hope. "They found her. She was still alive."

"Did they catch him?" Her eyes sparked with need.

He shook his head. "No, but they're searching. No." He reacted to her tensing. "Don't worry, just rest." With his other hand, he stroked back her hair. Her eyelids dipped once then stayed closed as she drifted into a restorative sleep.

Mac didn't dare take his eyes off her. Though her vitals had all returned to normal and the doctor had assured him that, though exhausted, she was fine. That she was sleeping peacefully and her body just needed rest to rejuvenate.

Still, he couldn't seem to shake off the fear of losing her. Now it was all settled down, it was worse because he had nothing to keep his mind from dwelling on all that had happened. How she had burned with fever at a dangerous level and how shallow her breathing had become.

He never wanted Laken to go through that experience again. He never wanted to go through that again. They had to catch the killer.

They'd come so close to getting him because of Laken, but The Hunter had managed to slip away. He had to get him. He tried to force his mind to go over everything they knew. Unfortunately, it wasn't much.

The man was careful, but he had slipped up this time. The woman had managed to scratch him so they now had DNA evidence. And with one mistake, there was a chance at another. It could be that the killer was losing his control, which might give them an advantage, but it also made him more dangerous.

Time was ticking before The Hunter would kill again. Mac looked down at Laken. Dr. Shannon would be there soon, and he knew, if the other doctor agreed, she'd want to hypnotize Laken again. He also knew it had to be done, they needed to try to get more information, but the thought of her living through it again sent dread coursing through him.

He caught the faint flutter of her eyelids and leaned forward. She drew in a breath and stirred in the bed. He rubbed his thumb over her knuckles and was rewarded with a slight smile.

CB&O

Mac was sitting by her, with her hand locked in his, when she opened her eyes. He looked haggard, but the smile that he gave her reached to the deepest part of her heart.

"Is it that bad?" Laken's voice cracked with the words.

"You tell me. How do you feel?" He brought her hand to his lips.

She took a deep breath, getting a strong smell of hospital, but felt free after being at the police station. "Tell me first, am I under arrest?"

"No," he said firmly.

"Then I'm tired and thirsty." He was already reaching for the water before she finished the sentence. "Can I go home now?"

"They're going to hold you tonight, to be on the safe side. I'm afraid the police department is going to stress that so they don't get hit with a big lawsuit if you have a," he paused for the right word, "relapse."

"It must've been quite a show I put on."

"I'd say a lot of people are going to be thinking of it for quite a while."

"The woman?" The shake was back in her voice.

"She made it through surgery, but it's still too early."

"They really did find her?" She tried to pull herself up but fell back in the bed, weak.

"Easy." He leaned up over her, brushing back her hair

and cupping her cheek in his hand. "She was right where you described to me. You saved her. She wouldn't have lived if we hadn't gotten there so fast."

Elation pushed back some of the fatigue and lingering fear, leaving her with hope. "You mean that?"

"Yes."

Laken didn't know if she could quite believe that the awful images could really be for good. But then again, wasn't that why she had gone to the police that first day, a hope that she might be able to help. Her thoughts locked on it for a few minutes. Mac remained silent beside her.

"You're going to need me to go over it?" She finally looked at him.

His fingers still holding hers tightened. "Yes, when you're ready." He looked away then back to her. "Dr. Shannon will be here shortly. She wants to hypnotize you again."

Her chest constricted like steel bands were clamping down, so she could only nod in reply.

Mac seemed to pick up on her distress. "You don't have to do it."

Laken managed to shake her head, loosening the tightness in her throat enough to get the words out. "No, I want to help. At least, I need to try."

"I'll be right beside you." He squeezed down his hand.

Laken wanted to tell him that was one of the things she was afraid of. That after seeing the strange sickness that was part of her, that, maybe, he would not want her anymore. Pain echoed deep in her soul and must've shown on her face because Mac reacted.

"Laken." There was anguish in her name as it escaped him.

"I want it to stop." The words ripped from her.

His head came down to press his cheek against hers. "I know. I wish I could make it. More than anything I don't want you to have to face that again. I'm going to get him, I promise."

His declaration almost broke her resolve not to cry. "But what if it doesn't stop with that? What if I remain linked to him?" She let out the fear that she hadn't even wanted to think about in her own mind.

He lifted his head and looked down at her, so close their noses almost touched. "I have to believe that it will end it. That once we defeat him, it will be over." He paused and took a long deep breath and let it out. "If not, then we'll face it."

The tears she fought so hard against pooled in her eyes. One made it free to trickle down the side of her cheek. "Can you really mean that?" she choked out.

"Yes." There was no hesitation in his reply. "I mean actually that."

"I can't hold you to that." Pain ripped at her heart. "I can't make you go through that."

"You are not making me do anything. I am not going to lose you. You have become very important to me."

Laken shook her head, afraid to try to get words out. He was noble, but she couldn't lock him to the insanity of her dreams.

"Yes." He read her actions. "When I got shot, and knew I was going to lose being a policeman, I didn't know how I was going to go on. I was losing myself, because that was how I thought of myself. That was what I was. Not just who. But now I'm actually faced with it, it isn't so hard, because a police officer is not just all I am. With you, I'm something more. You're part of my heart. Part of what I am. Part of what I want to be. I can't lose you. I love you."

"Mac."

"I mean it, Laken. Finding you, I found what I was missing in my life."

Laken thought her heart would burst. "Mac–"

A knock on the door interrupted her.

"You look better," Dr. Shannon said, entering the

room. "How are you feeling?"

Laken didn't think she could begin to explain how she felt. She was a jumble of fear. Fear of The Hunter, that he would kill again. Fear that she would have to live with the violent images. Fear of what it would do to Mac and her love for him. So she went with the only thing she could. "Fine."

"I'd like to talk to you about what happened at the station if you feel up to it."

Laken nodded and stiffened her resolve. "I was just going to go over everything I could remember with Mac. Then if you want you can try hypnosis again." She fought to keep down the shivers that coursed through her body. Mac tightened his hold on her hand, letting her know he was there for her.

೮೮೮

Their fingers were still locked together an hour later when her temperature started to spike again. "No." She gasped air.

The doctor who had checked her out when they brought her into the emergency room leaned forward to check on her. He had elected to be in the room when Dr. Shannon put her under.

"Laken, I want you to relax. He can't hurt you. Do you understand me? I want you to describe to me what you see, everything you can."

"We are in the bar. The Marinette. I've been there before."

"What about him? Do you think he has been there before?" Dr. Shannon probed, and Laken seemed to concentrate on it.

"Yes, yes, he's been there. He knows his way around. He's back in the corner so he can see the whole room. He's watching the women. The first couple women aren't right, though he thinks they deserve to die."

Mac caught the psychologist's attention and the

128

woman nodded, understanding he wanted to know why.

"Why aren't they right?" Dr. Shannon asked the question.

"He's looking for something special. He's aggravated. He shouldn't have had to hunt. He knew who he wants to kill, but he can't get to her." Laken's breath seemed to catch. "There's a woman that looks like what he wants, but she seems to know her place and is properly submissive. He wants to kill, needs to kill. They deserve to die. It's all their fault."

"What is all their fault?" Dr. Shannon pressed.

She shook her head. "Everything," she cried out. "He found her. She has the look and how dare she turn up her nose and snub the man. She's the one. She must die."

"Her temperature's climbing," the doctor announced.

"Laken, you need to draw back from The Hunter. He cannot affect you. Do you hear me? You can see what he is doing but not feel it. It's all in the past."

Mac felt the breath freeze in his own lungs until her breathing eased, along with her temperature. Still, it was all he could do to remain quiet as Laken continued to tell them every detail of the hunt, moving them down the street to the parking garage and catching his prey.

"No. The knife." Laken screamed as the knife plunge down.

Mac tightened his hold at the sound of pain in the word.

"Laken." Dr. Shannon came forward and rested her hand on hers. "It's all right. It's over. Laken, she is alive. The woman is alive." The words seemed to have no effect on comforting her this time.

Her head tossed side to side on the pillow, her breath coming in shallow pants. "No, he needs to hunt, to kill. It was no good. She wasn't the one."

The people in the room exchanged looks.

"What do you mean she wasn't the one?" Dr. Shannon

probed.

"Not the one he wants to kill. The need isn't gone. It's my fault the need won't go away. My fault the kill isn't good. It should have been good. She deserved to die, but the relief won't come. It's my fault," she groaned. "My fault it's all wrong. My fault the relief won't come. It won't come, won't come until he makes it right. Not until he kills me."

Chapter Thirteen

Mac never knew he could feel so much fear. Even waking up in the hospital, groggy with pain, wondering if his leg was still there wasn't as bad as hearing Laken say she was to die. "No." There was no keeping back the word that slipped from him.

Dr. Shannon sent him a brief look but said nothing.

It was Laken that answered with a nod, as if in her hypnotized state she accepted what she didn't even know when awake.

"How do you know he's after you?" Dr. Shannon picked up the new line.

"He was there outside my apartment when the policemen were putting me in the car. He was watching. He was happy I was in trouble. I deserved it. But, he was mad too, because he couldn't get to me. That's why he needed to find another, but he wanted to kill me."

"Did you see him there, Laken? Can you describe him?"

Again, Laken's head shook.

"So you just felt him?" the psychologist pressed.

"Yes."

"Have you felt him watching you before?"

"Yes."

Laken's answer was like a blow to his stomach. It was all Mac could do to keep his rage in.

"When did you feel him before Laken?"

"He was outside my work when I quit. I felt his hatred.

It hit me so hard it almost took me to my knees. I was afraid."

When Mac started to speak, Dr. Shannon cut him off with the jerk of her hand. "But you didn't tell Mac?"

"I was going to, but then I decided it was foolishness. I couldn't prove he was there. I couldn't even pick him out when I looked for him."

Mac couldn't believe how blasé her voice sounded talking about a killer watching her. He wanted to do some ranting and raving himself. Her next words took most of the steam out of him. "Then, when Mac called, all I wanted was to hear his voice, and I forgot all about the fear. It seemed silly."

"Laken, do you think Mac would think it was silly?"

"No. He would take it seriously. He would be worried. I don't want to add any more problems on him. He has enough trying to find The Hunter."

"You think you are a hardship for him?"

"Yes. I always thought I was normal − boringly so. I wish I was that way still. I want to help him catch The Hunter, but I want the dreams to go away."

The doctor nodded in understanding. "You are afraid the dreams will make you lose Mac?"

"Yes. How could a man want a woman that sees murders? I'm afraid they're going to drive me crazy." Emotion slipped back into her voice.

"Laken, listen to me. You're not going crazy. I want you to understand that. And though the visions are bad, they can't hurt you. You can use them to help Mac. You must remember that. You can use them to get The Hunter. And then the visions can end. Do you understand that?"

"Yes."

"Good. When you awaken, you will remember everything clearly. You will not feel fear in remembering, but the details will be clear in your mind. Do you understand?"

"Yes."

When Laken opened her eyes, she drew in a deep breath and looked for Mac. He was still beside her, holding her hand. The smile he gave her sent relief flowing through her body. "How did I do?" She forced a smile and then realized she actually felt good.

"Wonderful." He brought her fingers to his lips.

The medical doctor stepped forward to check her out before anything else could be said. With a quick assurance that she appeared to be fine, he left the room and Dr. Shannon started in with her probing. How Laken felt? What she could remember and such? It was twenty minutes later she left, after instructing Laken to get some sleep.

It was Mac who let out a sigh when the door closed behind her. "Finally, we're alone," he said before leaning over to lay his lips to hers.

The kiss was tender, sweet and lingering. When he pulled back, it was only a couple of inches to smile down, then his head dipped again to kiss her. This time, the kiss was more heated, and when her arms came up around his neck, his hands worked their way behind her back to lift her to him for deeper access.

The world around them slipped away. There were only the two of them, and Laken wished it could be like that forever. As if in agreement to that thought, Mac held her tighter. Heat shot through her body for a totally different reason than it had earlier.

A sound of an alarm in the hallway and the clattering of trays pulled them apart.

"I could really get addicted to doing that." Mac's voice rumbled down, making her want to laugh with sheer giddiness.

"I kind of like it myself. Anyone ever tell you, you're a pretty good kisser, detective?"

"I don't go around kissing many people on the job." His lip quirked up on one side, giving him an adorable dimple that Laken had only caught fleeting glimpses of before.

"So I'm a special case." Her own lips tilted up.

"Very special, a case totally by yourself."

"Is that good?" She got into the playfulness.

"Yes, I've decided I need to keep personal surveillance on you." The playfulness in his words didn't quite mask the seriousness underneath. Mac was letting her know he was going to be around to protect her, and it came clearly into her mind why.

"The Hunter is really going to come after me?" The light banter faded away.

"I'm not going to risk it." This time, when he pulled her back to him, it was more for comfort. "I won't lose you. Does that sound overly-dominating?" His lips brushed the side of her head as he asked.

Laken made only a slight negative motion. "No, you're a protector. That's who you are, and I think I'm kind of glad. It scares me to think he might come after me."

"Why didn't you tell me?" There was frustration in the words.

"I don't know. It seemed so ... outlandish. I already sounded like a fruitcake, and then to claim he was going to come after me. It would've made me sound paranoid or even a bigger nutcase. It was enough that you took my visions seriously. I didn't want to destroy that by sounding like an overwrought, hysterical female." She paused and leaned back to look up at him.

Reaching up, she cupped her hand on the side of his face. "I don't want to lose you," she repeated his words back to him. "Mac."

She swallowed back the tears that seeped into her eyes. "I love you. It's so fast, but you mean more to me than anyone ever has. I've never been one to fall in and out of love. I realized a long time ago that was not me, in fact I was beginning to wonder if I'd ever fall in love, but I decided to wait for it, to wait for you." She bit down on her lip to steady her nerves. "I've waited a long time for you and with these crazy things happening to me, I was afraid I'd lose you before I ever had a chance."

His hands came up to frame her face. "I'm not going anywhere. I'm not worried about a few off-the-wall visions except for what they do to you. They're not going to chase me away. Understand? I love you. We will face the visions together."

His thumb brushed away a tear that slipped free as joy spread through her. He loved her and wasn't going to leave. Happiness wiped away all her doubts and lingering fears.

⚬⚬⚬

Fear slashed through her as she stared into her small apartment. From the open doorway, she could see the destruction spread to every corner of it.

"Stay here in the doorway so I can still see you." Mac stepped in the room. His gun was in hand, his body tensed, alert. He scanned the room quickly before moving through the doorway to her bedroom.

He was out of her view for a second then he was striding back toward her, his gun once more in its holster. He didn't need to say no one was there. Whoever had torn apart her apartment was long gone.

Mac wrapped his arms around her, pulling her to him, cutting off her view of the mess, but she couldn't help picture the scattered items strung all over the room. She slumped against Mac, absorbing his strength, barely conscious of him talking on his phone.

This couldn't be happening, not after everything else. To have her apartment broken into, it was just getting too much. She wanted to scream. She wanted to pound her fist on something. Instead, she locked them onto Mac's shirt and clung to him as she was trying to cling to her sanity. She rubbed her cheek against his shirt to wipe away a tear she didn't even realize was there.

His arms tightened, making a comforting cocoon. His body gently rocked back and forth. The action actually brought a smile up through the hurt and conjured the image of him doing the similar thing to comfort a hurt child. It was such a pleasant picture she sighed and relaxed, letting go of all the pain of having her apartment trashed.

It was all right. Nothing was there that couldn't be replaced, she told herself and mostly believed it, but there was still pain and a feeling of violation. Her mind ran with that idea to the thought that having her apartment broken into was nothing compared to having a psycho-murderer invade her mind. She almost laughed at the absurdity of it. The sound that escaped her was more like a hiccup.

Mac's hand stopped stroking her back to catch her shoulders and ease her away to look down into her face. "You okay?" A frown knitted his brow.

The smile she gave him was slightly forced, full of mirth, but she did feel lighter so she told him why. "Yeah, compared to having a killer in my mind, this should be nothing."

The corner of his lip tugged up. "Well, I wouldn't say nothing, but you do have a point."

"Can I go take a look around and see what was stolen?" Laken stiffened her shoulders. "I need to call my insurance agent to see what they will cover."

"It'd be better to let the crime team go through it first." He held her back.

"Mac?" She saw the intensity in his face and looked past him, taking a really good look and knew what was going through his mind.

Her TV was still where it belonged, but the screen was broken out. Her CD player was on the floor. Though neither were new or expensive, they'd have still been worth money. She started to shake, really studying the room. Nothing appeared to be stolen. Trashed was the word that described it. Whoever broke in had been venting rage. She shuddered with relief that she hadn't been there.

Mac's arm tightened around her. "Come on, we can wait downstairs in the car."

"No." Laken held him back when he would've turned her. "I can handle this. Do you think it was The Hunter?"

The look in his eyes was serious. "I don't know. You have ticked off a couple people lately." His lips quirked into a grin which helped to ease the tightness that formed in her stomach.

"I don't think I can see Malcolm Warner breaking into my apartment to smash things up. I'd say it's a little beneath him. I don't think he'd go into a building like this even if his company designed it."

Mac nodded, accepting her comment but simply said, "You never know. But I will check it out. Let's see if your neighbors heard or saw anything while we wait."

☾⊗☽

Laken was exhausted when they stepped into Mac's apartment. Just inside the door, she slumped against the wall, closed her eyes and sighed in relief. The report had taken forever. She had expected just an officer to come and take her statement.

Instead, there was a team of two people that went over every square inch of each room. Laken knew why. Mac suspected it was The Hunter who had trashed her apartment and was hoping to find something that would lead to him. The more Laken thought about it though the more certain she became it was not The Hunter. There was no feeling there, but then again, maybe there wouldn't be if he was gone. Still, it seemed like she should know.

As it was, they didn't find anything except for the few dust bunnies she'd missed in her out-of-work, cleaning rampage before she'd been taken to the police station. None of her neighbors had noticed anything. Even Ardith Simmons across the hall, who never missed anything, for once was not at her post because the evening before she had been to an old friend's birthday celebration and that morning at a doctor's appointment.

She heard Mac close the door and put down her overnight bag. A second later his arms wrapped around her like they had earlier, and she was once again sheltered from the world. There were no tears this time when she rubbed her cheek against his chest. She was only aware of hard muscle and pleasant masculine smell accented with a touch of sandalwood. She breathed in deep. She liked his scent.

His hands ran up and down her for a second in a muscle relieving massage before Laken suddenly found herself being lifted into the air.

"Mac." Her eyes flew open as her arms locked around his neck.

"Easy, I'm not going to drop you. I can make it to the couch."

"I didn't think you would. I feel safe in your arms. It's … I've never had a man pick me up before you. It startled me." She let her fingers play with the edges of his hair. "I didn't mean to seem so helpless. I'm just so tired."

"Well." He eased her onto the couch. "You sit right here and rest. I'll see what we're going to have for dinner."

"You don't need to do that. I can help." She started to get up but he pushed her back down, sitting down on the edge of the couch beside her.

"You know, I've noticed that you don't let people take care of you very easily." He brushed back her hair.

"I don't mean to be difficult. I guess I've always been independent. My father raised my sister and me, so we were as capable as my brothers at doing things. My mom insisted that we learn to be ladies, and my brothers to act like gentlemen."

"I'll have to give my compliments to your parents then, because I think they did a pretty great job."

"Thank you."

"So, do you think your parents will like me?" His

finger dropped to brush her cheek in a slow caress.

"Oh yes. I think you are just what my parents hoped I would fall for." The words were airy as his head dipped toward her.

"And have you fallen?" he said huskily.

Laken found herself lost in the intensity of his eyes. They burned in her, and there was no hiding the truth. "Yes." Her heart thundered in her chest, wiping away all the weariness from her body. She felt charged from the electricity of being so close to him. "I love you."

Fire leapt in his eyes in reply. The hand on her chin slid behind her neck to cradle her head, holding her as he closed in. "I want to hear those words every day for the rest of my life. I love you." The words were sealed with the union of their lips. The kiss lingered for several minutes before he eased back, brushing lightly across her cheek before he broke contact. "I'm supposed to be letting you rest." There was no remorse in his tone.

"I prefer this. I feel much better," Laken added full-heartedly.

"Still." He stood, took a couple steps back from the couch and shoved his hands down in his pockets. "You lay here and relax. I will see what we have to eat, and no arguments." His words were meant as an order, but it was his eyes that kept her there. The need in them was so strong she couldn't move. He stared at her with hot intent for another minute before he turned away.

Laken's eyes followed him as he opened the fridge and set a few things on the counter before he crouched out of view. She heard him shift a few pans as her eyes wander around the room. It hit her that she was in love with a man, and this was the first time she had ever been in his apartment. They had always gone to her place for some reason. She was surprised at his apartment. It was tidy and very orderly but comfortable.

A brown suede chair sat against one wall. It looked

comfortable enough to nap on but she figured he spent more time in the rust-colored recliner from its position in front of the large TV mounted on the wall.

A stylized metal basket and a couple magazines and a book from one of the best-selling thriller authors sat on the entertainment table. There were two bookshelves filled with books showing a wide variety of interests. The most appealing thing Laken found was it all appeared to be dusted.

Soft music started bringing her attention back to him. He stood watching her from across the room. "Dinner will be ready in about ten minutes. It's one of those throw everything together and heat. My specialty."

"Do you like to cook?"

"I don't mind it. I like to eat. I'm finding I like it better when I have someone to do it with." He left it hanging that he meant her.

Laken got the message loud and clear from his eyes.

"If you want to wash up, the bathroom is through there."

Two hours later, Laken lay in Mac's bed thinking of him out on the couch. He had insisted that she sleep in his room, using the excuse that he had work to do and she needed a good night's sleep. But she knew that was just Mac being Mac. He had this strong sense of honor that was liberally laced with chivalry.

She sighed into the pillow and drew in a breath filled with his scent. It was all around her giving her comfort, just as the feel of him did. She could picture his arms around her and wished it was so.

She tried to close her eyes and will sleep to come. All she could think of was Mac. He loved her. Funny how that thought could make all the bad things going on around her meaningless.

She lay there for a few minutes more, than gave up on sleep. She wanted Mac, just to be near him, and it wasn't for security. It was because, well, it was just because. She pushed back the blanket and stood. Looking down at the satin T she wore to bed, she went to his closet and found a pair of sweatpants and a T-shirt and pulled them on, figuring he wouldn't mind.

Mac was sitting in the chair, his feet up, looking over a file of papers in his lap. She almost reached him before he looked up. When he saw her, he quickly closed the file and dropped it on the floor by the chair. "I thought you were sleeping. Nice outfit." He looked her up and down, raising his eyebrows, a grin kicking up the corner of his mouth, the dimple sneaking in an appearance.

"Do you mind?" She shifted back and forth, coming to a stop in front of him.

"You look incredible." He opened his arms.

She accepted the invitation and settled carefully in his lap. "I'm not hurting you?" she asked when he shifted her.

"No. I just want you closer. It's kind of nice to wrap my arms around you."

"Think you could get used to it?"

"Oh yeah." He brushed her hair back, caressing her cheek. When he cupped her face, she turned her head, pressing her lips into his palm. There was a growl in his voice when he spoke again. "I've been sitting here trying to work, but all I can think of is you. I love you, Laken. I want to marry you."

"Mac." His name burst out of her as his words reached her heart.

Before she could say anything else he groaned, tilting his head back, his eyes going to the ceiling. "I did not just propose to you, sitting in a chair, in my apartment, without even a ring." Anguish echoed in his words.

Laken's lips twitched up. "Yes."

He groaned again and she felt such love for him. She reached up and cupped his cheek, tilting his head back down to look at her. "Yes," she repeated, looking deep in his eyes. "I would love to marry you." There was no doubt in her. He was the only man for her and she wanted to be with him forever.

Chapter Fourteen

"I love you." She let the inner feeling shine through so there was no doubt she meant it.

She wasn't sure who made the move but their lips met in a kiss that sealed them together as assuredly as if they had just said their marriage vows. When they parted, his thumb caressed her cheek, his eyes drifted over her in wondering awe.

"Yes," was all he said before he cuddled her down against him. His arms locked around her, holding her to him. One hand burrowed into her hair, pressing her head to his shoulder as he rocked the chair back. His other hand ran up and down her back in a soothing motion. "Sleep now," he whispered, dipping his head to kiss her forehead. "All is how it should be and you need rest."

Laken wanted to say she was too excited to sleep. She was going to marry him, but the words were lost in a sigh, not making their way out as she, indeed, did fall asleep.

附

Mac felt contentment as he drew in a deep breath and was filled with the unmistakable fragrance of Laken. He started to stretch and froze. It wasn't that he realized he'd fallen asleep in his chair that halted him, that was a common enough occurrence. What was not common was the weight of the woman alongside him. He shifted carefully, trying not to disturb her but, so he could look down at her. She was nestled on her side, his arm wrapped around her, her head resting on his shoulder. Her face turned up to him as in an offering. An offering he longed to take, but he didn't want to wake her.

Laken looked so incredibly beautiful. She was wearing one of his T-shirts and sweatpants. He could barely make out a pair of thick, fuzzy socks on her feet next to his own stocking-covered feet. He ran his eyes back up over the length of them to her face and knew such desire to taste her pale pink lips that this time he couldn't stop himself from lowering his head to take the gentlest sip. It filled him with such pleasure he wanted to shout, wanted to claim more. Again, he held himself back.

Now was not the time. Too many things had to be resolved before it would be. Then his mind thought back on the evening before and his blurted-out proposal. He wanted to groan at the bungled way he did it, but smiled when he remembered she had said yes.

She hadn't just said it. She had meant it. It glowed there deep inside her as was his love for her. She would marry him and love him for the rest of her life as he would her.

He could be patient for her, and he would ask her again. Though it wasn't needed, he would ask her again, and he'd have a ring and flowers. He'd make it perfect – as romantic as any woman could dream of. But for now, he would bask in the pleasure of just holding her.

When desire threatened to take control of his mind, he forced his thoughts back to the case, and by the time Laken stirred in his arms. He had a new plan of action.

He was studying her again when she breathed in deep. His eyes almost crossed with desire when she rubbed her cheek against his shoulder then stretch along the entire length of him. Unable to resist her siren's call any longer, he promised himself only one kiss before he dipped his head to greet her lips. It was only one kiss, but as she woke to him, it blossomed into an incredibly drawn out, heated one. It was all he could do to release her.

"Good morning." He growled, wanting nothing more than to continue to devour her.

"That's not just good morning. Oh my." She blew out a breath and took another deep one to fill her lungs. "Oh, are you going to wake me up like that every day after we're married?"

"Well." He tried to look thoughtful. "I wouldn't object if you woke me up like that sometimes. But for now," he pressed the footrest down, sitting them upright so fast he had to hold on to her to keep from dumping her on the floor, "time to get moving."

"I liked where we were," she grouched bringing a smile to his lips.

"She does have a testy side, that's good to know. The problem is, I do too. That's why I'm going to go take a shower while you go fix me breakfast."

"Breakfast, and why do I have to do it by myself?"

"Because I made dinner last night, that's fair."

"Save me some hot water." She turned to the kitchen good-naturedly. She almost stumbled when she heard the words that followed her.

"There will be plenty of hot water because I'm going to have to make mine cold."

She turned slowly to look back at him.

"Go on, sweetheart, I'm hungry." He left it open to which hunger he wanted her to contemplate, and contemplate she did.

Since Laken couldn't keep her thoughts away from marrying Mac, she had a whole gambit of things to think about, but as they got ready to leave his apartment, her mind switched focus to the problem of finding the killer. She had actually figured Mac planned to leave her tucked away in his apartment, which would've been fine because she did feel safe there, and he had plenty of books to read to keep her busy. She was totally surprised when he said he was taking her with him.

"Where are we going?" she asked as he turned out of the garage.

"To your office building."

"Why? You really can't think it was my boss that broke into my apartment."

"No. I want to see what kind of security cameras are around the front of the building. You said you felt The Hunter watching when you quit. I want to see if we can find someone that fits your description of his build who was paying a lot of attention to you that day. That is, if we're lucky enough that the cameras haven't been cleared yet. A lot of places work a week loop, so we might get lucky and still be in time for a look, if we have a good angle."

"You think we might actually see him."

"It's a long shot but worth a try. I just hope we can get permission to view the video. Otherwise, we'll have to try for a warrant, and I'm not sure how that would go without solid proof he was there."

Laken missed what he said next as she felt spears of hope and dread go through her simultaneously. Could they find him? The thought had never occurred to her that a security camera might have caught him, or they might have a chance to pick him out. She prayed that it might actually be possible.

Mac's badge got them right in to see the chief of security. They were told the recordings from that day were still there, and when Mac told them what they hoped to find, it didn't take them long to get the clearance from the building manager.

Three cameras covered the front of the building. It took only a couple minutes since they had a very close approximate time for Mac to catch the image of Laken coming out. He had the manager slow the picture down, and watched Laken, vivid even in black and white. Righteous indignation showed upon her face as she confronted her boss and handed over the blueprint.

He heard the hitch of her breath from beside him as she watched herself turn back to the building, and Mr. Sherman catch her and hand over his card. There was awe and exaltation on her face as she moved to open the door, then she faltered, almost going down.

The camera again caught a view of her face, and this time, it was filled with terror. Her head turned back to study the crowd. Several people came up behind her, and she managed to stumble through the door, but her attention remained on the outside for several minutes before she finally forced herself away.

"That's what we want." Mac forced his attention from her image on the screen to other people in view. "Can you back it up just a little and go through it frame by frame?"

The scene on the sidewalk had drawn attention from several men. Mac saved pictures of each person they could see. Almost two hours had passed and they were on the third and final camera angle when a man in the top corner of the screen caught his attention.

Even though the man was back in the shadows, Mac could tell he was riveted by what was happening. As Laken moved back to the door, the man shifted to watch her. When she turned to look back, he pulled back, stepping behind a passing person, turning away so not to be noticeable, but he didn't leave.

"Got him!" Elation burst from within Mac. "I think I've got him."

Laken jerked beside him, her attention shifted from the section she was studying, and the security chief jumped up from the terminal where he was doing his own work to lean over the back of the chair.

"Watch." Mac backed up the video. "Now look at this guy here." He pointed to the screen and played it forward in slow motion.

When the man obviously dodged back, he heard a

catch in Laken's throat. Mac played it a second more before he reached up to freeze the recording. He turned to her even more certain. "What do you think?"

Laken's hand had come up to cover her mouth. Her eyes had a glassy, fearful look to them. He caught hold of her other hand that was balled tight. Her knuckles were white. "Laken," he said her name softly, stoking his thumb over her fist.

Her eyes came from the screen to him. She swallowed hard and shuddered. "I don't know. He's in the shadows, and I didn't get a very good look at him that night. He had a raincoat on, but I think it could be possible."

Her eyes went back to the frozen image, and she visibly shook. Mac could feel the fear in her and knew, though they had no proof, he was their man. That was The Hunter. He wanted to pull Laken into his arms. To take her away where she didn't have to think of killers and danger, but he had work to do now. His own thrill of the hunt filled him.

He turned back to the security chief. "Can I take this to see if our tech can come up with a cleaner image?"

The man started nodding even before he finished the question. "It's already been approved that if you found anything interesting, you'd take it."

"Thanks."

"You really think that's the guy?" He looked to the screen, then to Laken and back to him.

"Yeah, I do. Now we just have to identify him."

CŒBO

A half hour later Mac was repeating the same words to his captain. He knew it was a stretch for his superior to accept it without any evidence. But, after what he witnessed with Laken, he gave his approval for priority tech time to try for a clearer image that they could use for identification.

Captain Carter looked out his office window to where

Laken sat at his desk. "Has she ..." The man paused, pursing his lips to give himself time to go over his words. "...seen any more visions?"

"No." Mac shook his head. "You have the full report and tape from Dr. Shannon."

"Yeah, our victim is still hanging in there. The doctors still aren't saying for positive, but they say it's looking up with each hour that passes." The hand at his side clenched. "I want this guy." A stony, mean-business attitude settled over the captain and he left it at that.

Mac didn't need more. He wanted the killer more than anyone there. He looked out at Laken. It was personal for him.

The captain switched subjects behind him. "The tech got a lot of prints off her apartment, but there was no match. So whoever did it hasn't got any priors, and I'd say was ticked off enough to not be thinking clearly enough to worry about prints."

Mac thought for a minute before he turned back. Icy certainty filled him. "It wasn't The Hunter. He's too methodical. He wouldn't blow like that, unless he's really losing it. I can't see him far gone enough to not wear gloves like he has so far."

He was quiet a minute more, thinking it through in his mind. "I think gloves are part of his MO, not just so he doesn't leave evidence. It's that he doesn't want to get his hands dirty with them. They're beneath that to him. It's what he's proving. They're not as good. Beautiful, but back stabbing. Steps on them, again it's because they're beneath him. He's going to trod them under, when he's done with them."

"It fits, and I concur about the apartment. Though, you do realize that means someone else isn't happy with your girlfriend?"

There was no need for the captain to point it out. Mac had figured that out before they had left there the day before. So he simply nodded. "I can't leave her alone, unprotected." He figured he didn't need to say not only was she the only witness they had, but what she meant to him personally, and he was right.

It was the captain's turn to nod. "You're going to keep her around here while you work?"

"Yeah."

"If you have to follow something up or she wants to go home, grab an officer to put on her. I'll okay it for now."

"Thanks."

"All right, back to work."

Mac reached for the door, but the voice behind him stopped his hand on the knob.

"Get this guy, Mac."

He looked back over his shoulder. "I will." It was an easy promise to make, and in that instant, he realized they both knew it would likely be the last big act of his career. Looking to the woman waiting for him at his desk, he could honestly say he didn't mind as long as it meant he got to spend the rest of his days with her.

He steeled his shoulders. That meant he needed to find The Hunter – fast. *"Not until he kills me."* The unwanted words came to his mind. He wasn't going to let that happen. Laken was his. The Hunter had picked the wrong prey this time because he wasn't getting her.

Laken stood as he approached her. "What did your captain say?" Anxiety poured off her.

"We're going with the video. They'll get working on it right now. It might take some time though. So until then I follow up other leads."

"What about me?"

"For now, you stay here with me."

She nodded. "I need to go home sometime to start cleaning up."

"I'll get an officer to take you home in a little while if that's okay."

A shudder passed over her, but she nodded again. "You think it's necessary?"

"I'm not going to take chances." He reached out and caught her hand, giving her fingers a squeeze. "You okay here?"

"Yeah, I raided your bookcase before we left." She pulled a book from her bag.

It was one of his favorite authors. "That's a good book."

"I like him, but haven't read this one yet," she came back.

"It's a good time then." He directed her to a chair and hoped the adventures of Dirk Pitt could keep her mind from her own real life and death battle.

It was only about an hour until the end of his shift when Jonesy came up with a lock on one of the guys they had been checking out. He had dated the first victim, and she'd reportedly dumped him because her job was taking off, and he didn't take it very well. Mac didn't like letting Laken out of his sight but agreed to let an officer take her home.

Fifteen minutes later, Laken stood in her doorway and sighed. It was all she could do to keep the tears from surfacing. Her neat little apartment was an absolute wreck.

Behind her Jeffers, the officer escorting her, let out a low whistle. "I'd say someone was tick off. You okay, ma'am?"

Laken drew in a deep breath and squared her shoulders. "Yeah." She knew what to expect, but it wasn't much easier than it had been seeing it the day before. Tentatively she stepped through the doorway. "I'd say make yourself comfortable but that might be hard."

"It's okay. What can I do to help?" the man volunteered.

"Well, first I need to call my insurance company and make sure I can start cleaning up." It only took a couple minutes before she was assured that the adjustor had been out. He had all he needed, and her claim was being processed.

So they set to work up-righting undamaged things. To the side of the door they made a pile of broken items and sacks of her possessions that had been reduced to garbage. Laken held the pieces of a small horse statue that she'd gotten as a birthday present when she was about ten and horse crazy. She bit her lip to keep tears back. With a sigh she dropped it into the garbage bag.

A knock on the door made her jump, her hand going to her heart. It took a second to calm herself before she moved toward it, but the officer motioned her back, positioning himself beside the door before she looked through the peephole.

Laken let out the breath she hadn't even realized she was holding. "It's Mrs. Simmons. She lives across the hall." When he nodded and stepped back, she took a second to steady herself and opened the door.

"Hello, Mrs. Simmons."

"Oh, Laken, it was you I heard. I feared it was a burglar when I heard a racket in here."

Laken wasn't fooled. She was positive the woman had known it was her all along. She had just waited until she couldn't stand it any longer before her nosiness drew her to cross the hall. "Sorry we disturbed you. We're just trying to clean up."

"Oh, pish posh. It is so unbelievable. To think this could happen here. I'll tell you, it makes me so nervous. Howard agreed to stay with me a couple extra days until my nerves settled down. He is such a good boy. When are you going to go out again?"

Laken wondered what Howard had told her. Obviously, it didn't entail the truth about how the date went. "Actually, I've met someone else, and we've become serious." There was no way she was going to let her know that Mac had asked her to marry him.

Mrs. Simmons was nice and meant well, but she was a huge gossip. And, she hadn't even had a chance yet to call her family and tell them she was engaged. Thoughts of Mac brought a wave of reassuring warmth through her.

The woman glanced at the police officer, who was keeping a discreet eye on her from the kitchen, then turned back to her. "That nice man you were with the other day, the one that brought you flowers?"

It hit hard when the woman said flowers, except for one she had pressed in a book to save, the rest were sticking out of the garbage with the vase she had put them in. "Oh well, yes."

"He did seem very nice. A little rugged though, don't you think?"

Laken could almost see the woman figuring how to work her nephew back in, not that Laken was going to let that happen. "You don't happen to have a couple boxes do you, Mrs. Simmons?"

The woman jerked, obviously caught by surprise. "Oh yes, dear, of course. I should've thought. The broken glass. It really doesn't go in trash bags very well."

"Yes," Laken agreed.

"If you'd like to come get them, I think I have at least three or four." Mrs. Simmons turned to her door.

Laken looked back over her shoulder at the policeman. "I'm going across the hall to get some boxes."

The man frowned, concern creased his brow. "Leave the doors open so I can see you."

Laken nodded, feeling that it sounded excessive, but not willing to take any chances. She followed Mrs. Simmons. Her apartment was a two bedroom, one of the bigger units in the building. Still, it felt cramped with all the woman's knickknacks.

The older woman had a special fondness for porcelain cats and dogs. They each had names, and she pampered them as if they were real, which Laken thought was funny until one day the woman confided she was extremely allergic to animals but always wanted a pet.

"I just shudder at the thought of someone getting in here and breaking my babies." The woman trailed her hand fondly over a life-sized basset hound.

"Fortunately, I didn't have anything like your collection, and I don't think you have anything to worry about. I'm sure it was just a one-time thing, and I was just the unlucky one it happened to."

"But the policeman there?"

"Oh, he's a friend of a friend." Laken gave the first excuse she could come up with, not willing to tell the old woman she might have a killer after her. "He just offered to help."

"I see. That was nice. Well, there are a couple boxes in the corner in there if you want to get them. I think there's one more in my closet."

The woman turned into her room, and Laken headed for the spare bedroom. She was almost through the door before she noticed Howard stretched out on the bed his hands behind his head. His shirt unbuttoned and the tails hanging free.

"Well, this is a nice surprise." The man's eyes moved over her in an insulting manner.

Laken paused, then forced herself forward, seeing the boxes. "I'm sorry to disturb you. Ardith didn't say you were here. I was just getting some boxes."

She picked them up, but when she turned back, Howard was no longer on the bed but stood between her and the door. A wave of fear hit her, but she pushed it away. "If you'll excuse me."

"You still think you're all that. Coming on so prim and proper." The man ground out in a low, menacing tone. "But you're not. You're as two-faced as any other. Giving it to that other guy, aren't you? Noticed you were gone the last couple nights."

A sneer pulled up his lips, and his eyes tightened with threat. "And now you come in here. What, did you find out he wasn't any good after all? Women are liars and cheats. All of you just want what you can get. Well, I guess I could give you some if you ask real nice." He stepped forward.

Laken backed up, lifting the boxes between them as a shield. "Excuse me. I need to go."

"What do I have to do? You like coaxing?"

"I'd like to go. Your aunt is just in the other room."

"If I close the door, she won't disturb us," he challenged and Laken took it up.

"Yes, but there's a police officer in my apartment, and if you close that door, he will disturb us. Now back off before I yell."

The man seemed to think on her words a second then dismissed them, taking another step forward, forcing her back against the wall.

The feel of it behind her gave her strength. "I mean it, Howard. I tried to be nice to you because of your aunt, but if you don't back off, I'm going to hit you, then I'm going to start screaming."

"You wouldn't hit me."

"Oh, yes I would." The force behind the words must have finally sunk in.

He scowled and swore. "Ice queen. Think you can take on a man?"

"I don't want to take you on. I want to go. Now let me pass." She shoved forward with the boxes, bumping him to the side. She was almost passed him when his hand locked on her arm. Laken didn't think, just drove her elbow back into his stomach. The hand released her, and the man doubled over.

"Don't ever touch me or come near me again." She enunciated the words through clinched teeth. "The only reason I'm not yelling my head off for the officer is I happen to like your aunt, but I suggest you get some counseling. You need help in your relationships with women."

By the time Laken reached her apartment, she was remarkably calm. The anger Howard raised helped burn off some of the residual fears that still lingered in her mind.

A few minutes later, Mrs. Simmons dropped off the other box, obviously ignorant of any problem between her and Howard. Laken though, was not ready to engage in any more small talk and excused herself, saying she needed to get back to work.

The apartment was pretty much back in order when Mac showed up.

"You've been busy." He eyed the clean room and the boxes and bags stacked by the door along with her TV and sound system. "Looks like we need several trips to the dumpster."

"Yes." She sighed. "I only have a handful of dishes that weren't broken. Officer Jeffers has been a great help." She smiled back at the man.

"You're welcome, ma'am. You taking over now?" He looked to Mac.

"Yes, you're relieved. Thanks."

Jeffers nodded and, after a thank you from Laken, he left.

Laken turned from the door to find herself caught up in Mac's arms. "Oh," the word slipped out right before his lips settled on hers.

"Hello there," Mac drawled out when he lifted his head. He lowered his face into her hair, taking in a deep breath of her. "It's nice to come home to you."

"I can agree with that." She gave him another kiss before they stepped apart. "I'm afraid I can't offer you much to eat."

"That's okay, I'll take you out." He studied her apartment again. "You've definitely been busy."

"It wasn't hard. Most of it was swept up into the garbage. Luckily, it looks like my renters insurance is going to come through and cover a lot of it."

"That's great." He placed a finger under her chin and tilted it up. "But it's still hard."

"Yes." She knew she was going to have to tell him about what happened with Howard, but it didn't make it any easier either. Still, she decided not to keep anything from him, though she doubted it had any relevance to what was going on. She was like a magnet for trouble lately. "You want to help me take some of this stuff down."

"Sure." He grabbed the biggest box, and she took a couple garbage bags.

She waited until they were in the elevator going down before she started to tell him what happened with Howard. Laken could see the temper rising in him before the elevator doors opened.

"Back up and tell me everything again," he ordered as she led the way to the dumpster, asking no other questions, just listening as she talked. They were back in the elevator when she couldn't take it any longer. "Mac, what are you thinking?"

Beside his leg, his fist clenched and unclenched again. "That I'd like to beat the daylights out of the man."

She reached out and caught his arm. "You are not going to beat him up."

"You sure?"

There was no mistaking the challenge in him. The ding of the elevator door opening had her shifting in front of him. Her other hand pressed against his chest, keeping him back. "You can't beat him up. Then you'd have to arrest yourself."

She moved closer. "Mac, I didn't tell you so you'd go after him. I told you because I promised myself that I would never keep anything from you. I really don't believe Howard has anything to do with the killings or my apartment. Do you?"

There was a brooding silence about him. The doors behind her closed at the same time his arms wrapped around her. He gave a gentle tug, pulling her against him. "For the record, I was not going to beat him up, no matter that I would like to. But, I am going to have a talk with him and run a check to be on the safe side."

She got no answer out before his mouth captured hers. They made it back to the ground floor before they had to break apart to move back to let a middle-aged couple get on. The woman gave them sly looks, and the man just grinned as they rode the three floors in the shared elevator.

Mac took the key from her and opened her apartment, and gave her a nudge inside. "Wait here, I'll be right back."

Laken reached out to catch his arm, but the answer to her unspoken question was already being delivered.

"Don't worry, I won't hit him." He closed and locked the door before she could add any further objections.

Chapter Fifteen

Mac forced the desire to hit the man down. Fortunately, it was his aunt that answered the door. He pasted his ever-handy cop smile on his face and greeted her before asking if her nephew was there.

"You want to speak to Howard?" Concern filled the woman's voice, making it go sharp, bringing the aforementioned man into the hall.

"Yes, just for a minute out here in the hall. Just checking on things he might have noticed the day Laken's apartment was broken into," Mac added.

"Oh, yes. He wasn't here when you talked to me earlier."

"No," Mac used the excuse, glaring over the woman, not giving her nephew a chance to back out. "If we could talk." Mac motioned out the door, and the man sullenly moved past.

Mac just closed the door when Howard started. "What's this? I don't know what the lying witch told you but nothing happened."

"Laken told me everything, and I want you to leave her alone. I will make that clear, but as I said to your aunt, I want to know if you saw or heard anything the day of the break in?"

"What? You think I had something to do with it? Did she say that? She's lying. I've never even been in her apartment."

"But you're not happy with her."

"She's a —" the man paused in mid-sentence, "— a tease."

Mac arched an eyebrow. "I guess we see things differently. I assure you, Laken doesn't play games like that, but that's beside the point. Laken is with me now so you don't have to worry about her."

"You're welcome to her. There are plenty of other beautiful women around."

"What I want to ask you about, is where you were three nights ago?"

The man looked lip locked for a second. "Why do you want to know?"

"Part of something I'm working on. You can answer me here or go down to the police station."

Howard shrugged, obviously disturbed. "I was with a secretary I met that day."

"Does she have a name?"

"Yeah, you might want it, but I don't think I'm sharing. She's a whole lot more fun." He looked past him to Laken's apartment.

Mac cut off the comment he knew was coming. "I need the name, in case we need to verify your alibi. Will she collaborate you story?"

It seemed to sink in on the man that he was serious. He shifted uneasily. "Yeah, we ate at the seafood place on Holmes. I still have the receipt. After that, we went back to her place. You're not going to pin anything on me." He jerked his thumb toward Laken's apartment. "Whatever she says I did, I didn't do it."

"Laken didn't accuse you of anything, but I'm telling you, stay away from her." Mac turned, using Laken's key to open the door, leaving the man standing in the hall.

Laken was waiting just inside the door and about pounced on him. "Mac!

He laughed, feeling a lot better than he had a few minutes earlier. "Do you want to check my knuckles?"

"What?"

He obviously took her by surprise and the wind out of her sails. "For scrapes."

"You hit him." She grabbed his hand pulling it up to inspect.

"No, I didn't hit him, though he probably deserved it. I'll just have to be satisfied that you elbowed him."

"Then you don't think he's behind any of it?"

Mac had to sigh at that. It sure would've been a heck of a lot easier, but he didn't. "No. I'll check him out, though. But, hey." He reached up and cupped her chin. "Don't worry, I'll get him."

"I know. It's just a lot. I'm tired."

"Well, let's take the rest of this stuff down to the dumpster then I'll take you out to eat."

"Sounds good." Laken grabbed the remaining garbage bag, while Mac stacked the two small boxes to take down. "I didn't ask you. Any leads pan out?" she asked as she held the door for him to precede her out.

"The one we followed up this afternoon was a wild goose chase, but the picture off the video is looking pretty promising. The guys did a good job cleaning it up. They're running it now to see if we can get any matches from possible priors. It's out to all units, and tomorrow we'll start canvassing the area around where you work to see if he works in the area."

"Because he was down there?"

"That, and because of the raincoat that you described him wearing each time hints to a business man and that is the main business area. It's a stretch, but if the guy follows the past, he won't wait long until he'll kills again. Dr. Shannon feels he's become very obsessive. Whatever triggered him, he went way off. He won't quit until he's stopped."

"So even if he kills me he won't stop," Laken said plainly.

The jolt of pain that hit him was now expected but wasn't any easier to take. "I'm not going to let that happen."

Laken pushed back against the doors that let them out to the dumpster, facing him as he stepped out. "I know."

"We're getting closer, Laken, I can feel it."

"Yes."

Mac tossed the boxes into the overflowing bin. He'd just taken the garbage bags from her when the internal blow hit her. She stumbled, barely catching the filthy metal of the dumpster to keep her from going down. Her heart pounded in her chest and echoed in her head. Her breathing became rapid, but she couldn't seem to get any air into her lungs. Lights flashed in front of her eyes, and she felt herself start to pass out.

"Laken." Her name reached her through the searing thunder in her head. She clung to the sound of the voice as it called her again. She didn't know how long it had been before she could place the feel of Mac's arms around her, holding her to his body.

"It's okay, sweetheart, I have you."

"M–Mac?" Her breath still came in pants. The pounding in her heart and head eased. Awareness returned slowly to her. She forced in a lungful of air, counting to ten before letting it out and repeating the process.

When she shifted to steady herself, Mac leaned back to look down at her. "All right now?" His face was a landscape of concern.

She nodded.

"Another vision?"

This time she shook her head before she manage to stammer out her reply. "I'm not sure what it was. Anger, rage, hatred. It was from him but –." She shrugged. "I don't know. He's ... he wants to kill."

"You," Mac added what she hadn't.

"Yes. What I felt seemed to be all focused on me."

"Come on. Let's get you inside." He moved them to the building, and though his concern was on her, his attention was on his surroundings. He searched for signs of anyone watching them. He couldn't say he understood what happened to Laken but couldn't help wondering if what she felt was because The Hunter was close. Once he had her through the doors, he pulled out his cell phone and hit speed dial to Jonesy.

"Yeah," Jonesy answered sounding distracted.

"Can you get some units over to Laken's block, have them do some drive-bys to look for someone matching our guy?"

"She have another vision?" Jonesy asked, now sounding fully alert.

"Not really a vision, more like a sense, a feeling of rage. It was directed at her, and it was so strong it almost put her out."

"She okay? Do you need an ambulance?"

"No, she's okay." Mac glanced at her. "We're going to hold up in her apartment for about a half hour then I'll take her to get something to eat." He tightened his hold on her. She leaned weakly against him. Her body still had tremors racing over it, but they had eased.

"Okay, I'll let you know what they find. Why don't I pick up Connie and meet you at the fun center?"

"Sounds like an idea." Mac said, forcing his attention back to the phone. "See you there. Thanks."

In her apartment, Mac found a box of herbal tea and fixed her a cup as she sat on the couch wrapped in a blanket. Though it wasn't cold, she was chilled. He handed her the cup and settled down to cuddle her in his arms.

She took a few sips than placed the cup on the end table and turned into his body, resting her head on his chest. "You're better than the tea." Her arms worked their way around him. "I'm surprised you found a mug."

"It was the only one." He ran his hands over her back.

"I called Dr. Shannon while I was fixing the tea. She agrees he might be watching you. That could be why it was so strong. She warned that you shouldn't be alone. She believes he will come after you."

He let the words hang for a minute before he added. "And, she believes it will be soon. She doesn't think he's stable enough to wait long. That's in our favor because it will make him sloppy. You have to stay close."

"Maybe you could use me to draw him out."

Mac was shaking his head before she finished. "We don't do things like that. Hanging you out like a carrot is a good way to get you dead."

"But —"

"No, that's a TV stunt. Too many things could go wrong. I'm not going to risk it," he said adamantly.

"What if he goes after someone else because he can't get to me like last time?" She pulled back, pain filling her eyes.

"Dr. Shannon and I both agree that's unlikely. It didn't work for him last time. He wants you, only you. And he's going to come to us." There was no doubt in him.

"That puts you right in the way."

"And that's where I'm going to stay." His statement left no room for challenge.

Jonesy called about twenty minutes later to say the drive-bys didn't pick up anything. It didn't mean he wasn't out there watching. There were just too many places to hide.

Mac had been afraid that was going to be the outcome, but he'd hoped. The bigger problem would've been if they pick him up from the matching description. At this point, they didn't have enough evidence to tie him to the murders. Still, having a name and knowing who he was would be a big help.

Mac decided, for now, it was time to get Laken's mind off The Hunter and add some fun back into their lives.

Jonesy and Connie were waiting out in front of the Fun Center when they arrived. Laken was already smiling when Mac came around to get her out of the car.

"Hi," Connie greeted from ten feet off. "If you have any delusions that these two," she motion to Mac and her husband, "are grownups, they're about to be shattered."

"Hey," Mac shot back with mock indignation. "I'll have you know their Tex-Mex restaurant is pretty good." He greeted his friend's wife with a kiss on the cheek. "You just don't know what class is because you hang around this guy too much."

"That may be true." She winked and then turned back to Laken. "This is these two's stress-relief stop. They come here for the reaffirmation that there is good in life."

"That's right," Jonesy finally spoke up. "It doesn't get any better than bowling or glow-in-the-dark miniature golf."

After two games of bowling, Laken's appetite kicked in with a vengeance, and she learned that Mac's plea for a handicap, which was quickly shot down by Jonesy, was not needed. Over a burrito grande, which was no exaggeration in size, and an endless supply of chips and salsa, she felt more like her normal self. They joked, laughed, and she fell deeper in love with the man who, in two weeks, had become an incredibly important piece of her life.

Mac smiled over at her when she leaned back and groaned in satisfaction. "I told you it was good." He waved a chip in front of her nose.

"Not another or I'll explode. I can't believe I ate the whole thing."

"And, I'd calculate, two baskets of chips," he said pointedly.

She groaned again. "Don't remind me."

"Haven't you learned yet, Mac, you never point out how much a woman eats?" Connie shook her finger at him.

"Why? I like a woman with a healthy appetite. It's the

dainty, picky eaters that drive me up the wall. You know most of the time it's just pretense, and they're going to eat when you take them home after they waste a good meal that you paid for."

"That's what's nice about getting married," Jonesy said. "They eat in front of you, and the leftovers she takes home, you get to eat if you get to them first."

"Hmmm, never thought about that." Mac looked at Laken's empty plate. "Oh well, too late for that tonight. Ready?" He shifted his gaze to her.

"For what?" She looked wary.

"Miniature golfing."

"I don't think I can move." She let him pull her up.

"Come on, we'll make it interesting. Loser has to make the winner breakfast tomorrow." His eyes gleamed with challenge.

"You're on, just don't mention food again."

They were tied at the seventh hole when Laken's ball clipped the edge of an obstacle, sending it down a spiraling tunnel of neon lights into a side trap area instead of dropping down the hole to take it to a lowered platform like Connie and Jonesy's had.

Mac hooted with laughter, nudging her out of the way to place his ball down. "Watch a pro."

"Yeah, yeah," Laken returned.

"He talks so big," Connie said conspiringly.

Unfortunately, Mac's ball slid smoothly in the desired hole. He turned arching his eyebrows. "Breakfast."

"It's not over yet," Laken shot back. "I can still catch you. Just watch the ball come out down there and drop right into the hole." She sashayed off down the spiraling tunnel where her ball had disappeared.

"Maybe I better come make sure how many strokes it takes you to get it in the hole up here." Mac paused at the top of the slope that dropped to the hole.

Laken turned, walking backward up the ramp, and

wrinkled her nose at him. He laughed again, following the other couple down to the lower level. Laken was smiling when she turned the corner to find where her ball had disappeared.

She spied the ball against the wall in a small dip only about three feet from the hole. Laken glanced at the ball then the hole, taking her position to putt. A movement to the side startled her. She pulled back throwing up her arm in defense.

"Ma—" The scream that tried to leap out of her throat died against the hand that clamped over her mouth. The stench of alcohol assaulted her as the man's thick arm locked over her body, trapping her back against him.

Laken twisted her head, trying to rip free, only to have the hand on her mouth tighten down, digging her teeth into the soft flesh of her lips.

"It's all your fault." The words rippled in her mind with waves of fears.

Chapter Fifteen

No! Laken's mind screamed. I*t couldn't be him. It wasn't right. Couldn't be him.*

Stewart Hoster was the right height, but his looks were wrong. And besides, she'd worked directly under him for almost four years. She really didn't like him but had never felt fear around him.

The words tumbled over in her mind as it strived to take in the situation and make sense of it. Why would he kill those women? She went to shake her head only to be reminded of the arms locked around her.

"It's all your fault." The words repeated in her ear. "You just couldn't let things be." His voice was slurred, filled with hatred, but it brought no fever, no terror. It was like she didn't even feel him there, that she was totally detached from the situation. Her mind remained clear and calm.

The sound of voices coming through the spiraling tunnel reached her and she knew other people were there. All she had to do was get free long enough to yell and Mac would be there.

Hoster, too, must've become aware of the approaching people because he shifted suddenly, pulling her toward a shadowed corner where the neon light above it announced an exit. It sent her into motion as Laken felt her first real shot of fear. She couldn't let him get her out that door. Spreading her feet wide, she pressed her running shoes into the fake turf and felt them catch, halting their motion.

Behind her, Hoster cursed and tried to jerk her to the side to dislodge her. Laken shifted, keeping her feet wide, letting her body drop like a weight in his arms. Hoster had her by five inches, but the motion almost unbalanced him. He tried to lift her, but Laken struggled with her arms, getting enough freedom to jab an elbow back into his stomach.

The man grunted in pain, giving her encouragement. She fought harder. Throwing her head back, she caught him in the chin instead of the nose. The blow had her seeing stars but the hand over her mouth loosened. Shaking her head to the side, at the same time she twisted her body, she dislodged the hand from her mouth as he tried to hold onto her body.

The scream Laken tried for earlier burst over the music and the noise. Hoster didn't seem to care about her silence any longer. His whole attention was focused on holding her.

Laken slammed her head back again. This time she thought she might have connected with his nose. Whatever it was, the man swore. Shoving her away from him into the brightly painted wall. Pain ricocheted through her head. Stunned, her legs gave out from under her and she fell to the ground.

She caught the image of a hand reaching for her, but before it could lock on her it was ripped away as Mac rammed into him. The two men slammed to the wall only a couple feet from her. Laken got her head up in time to see Mac slam his fist into Hoster's jaw. The man dropped. Mac drew back his fist to let it go again, but Jonesy was there to grab his arm.

"He's had it."

Jonesy's words cut through into her mind as it must've Mac's because he slowly lowered his arm and turned to her. The anger softened from his face. He dropped to his knees, leaving Hoster to Jonesy, to catch her to him.

"Are you all right?" The words growled from deep within him as he cradled her head against his chest.

His heart thundered under her cheek. One hand stoked up and down her back while the other kept her tight. She clung to him but still forced herself to turn her head to look over at Hoster.

Mac must've felt the motion because he eased back enough to catch her chin and tilt her head back to look at him. "Don't worry about him. He's not going to hurt you or anyone else."

Again anger poured from him, but there was gentleness in his touch as he caressed her face. "I'm sorry. I never thought there'd be a chance to get to you here with so many people. I'm so sorry." He punctuated it with a kiss, breaking it to tilt his forehead to rest against hers. "You okay?"

"Yes." Laken soaked in the feel of him.

"You sure? I could've lost you. You did great, just the right thing fighting him." He kissed her again.

"I knew I couldn't let him take me away." She glanced toward Hoster, who was still on the ground.

Jonesy was now talking on his cell phone. A few people were gathered in the tunnel, curiosity plain on their faces.

A tremor of fear snuck its way over her, and Mac tightened his hold.

"It's okay," he said soothingly.

"I'm fine. I just can't believe it's him. It doesn't seem possible. I didn't feel anything from him. I still don't, no rage, nothing. At the pharmacy, I looked into his eyes, they don't seem right − not the same."

"Don't worry about it. It's −"

Whatever Mac was going to say was cut off by an officer running through the tunnel with one of the young men who worked there. They were followed a second later by another officer. Laken watched as Jonesy took the handcuffs from the officer and attached them to Stewart Hoster's wrists.

Her former boss was now fully conscious and shooting arrows of hatred at her but didn't say anything. He remained stoically silent while they read him his rights, only nodding at the end.

The absence of fear or the sickness The Hunter normally generated was almost a shock to her. With him caught, it looked like the nightmares were truly over. Mac stood to talk to the officers, and Connie took his place beside her, wrapping her arm around her shoulder.

One of the officers came over to ask for her statement. He was going over details when Mac headed back toward her, he stopped short, staying back. Laken could see the tension still radiating through him as he leaned back against the wall, eyeing her in undisguised concern.

As soon as the officer stepped away, Mac came forward extending his hand to draw her up into his arms. He hugged her so tight, it forced the air from her but nothing had ever felt so good. She was free from the nightmare. Free to love him.

"I'll take you to the hospital to be checked out. Then I have to go to the station to make a full report."

It was Laken's turn to pull back. "I don't need to go to the hospital. I'm not hurt." She could see his objection coming. "Please Mac. I'm okay. Just a couple bruises is all. I don't want to go to the hospital."

He was quiet a minute before he sighed. "All right, you can come with me, but I'll warn you, I don't know how long it will take with the reports and questioning."

"Why don't I take her back to our place?" Connie spoke up. "You won't need her anymore tonight, will you?" As if reading his hesitation, she added. "She can get some rest, and I'll keep an eye on her in case it looks like she needs to go to the hospital."

Laken was relieved when Mac finally agreed. Though

she wished she could have stayed with him, she really was exhausted and wanted nothing more than to get some sleep. Sleep that wouldn't be plagued with nightmares of death.

It was still another half hour before Mac walked her to Connie's car, and helped her inside, going so far as to do up her seatbelt before pressing her back into the seat with one final, hard kiss.

On the other side of the car, Jonesy gave Connie a kiss. "It'll probably be almost morning before we get there. We want to stay for the questioning. Get some sleep."

"We'll be okay," Connie assured him, dropping into the seat.

Mac stayed by the door, clearly debating on letting her go.

"Go." Laken smiled reassuringly, and waved him away. His gaze remained on her a moment longer before he closed the door.

Beside her Connie laughed. "You just got to love protective males. They are just so cute."

A rush of agreement burned through Laken as she watched Mac stare after them until they turned the corner.

The Jones's house was quaint, a bungalow style in a middle class neighborhood that screamed of family.

"This is beautiful," Laken commented as she followed Connie in.

"Thanks, just make yourself comfortable. It was a fixer-upper when we got it. The person had really let it run down so we got it for a song. Mac's put in a lot of hours helping us remodel it. It's nice to see him find someone, especially after the shooting. We've been worried about him, especially how he'd take the forced retirement."

"He's going for a teaching position at a university."

"I heard, I think that's great."

Laken shifted as warmth coursed through her. "Mac asked me to marry him."

The woman let out a squeal and hugged her. "Oh, my.

I presume you said yes?"

"Yes." Laken about burst with renewed excitement. "You don't think it's too soon?" She wondered what the woman would say, though she seemed happy.

"With Mac, no way. Mac is one of those men who knows what he wants. Besides, I've seen the way he is with you. You hit him hard from the very first. I'll admit, was worried when Marcus originally told me. He was real worried because Mac fell hard for a fruitcake. But after meeting you – you guys are perfect together." Connie gave her another hug.

After a cup of hot chocolate and girl talk, Laken settled into bed in the spare room and let sleep come to her through the lingering thoughts of Mac.

ೞಬೂ

Mac was at the point he wanted to slam his fist into the wall. He looked at the man who sat sniveling in the chair. There was no way he was The Hunter. He might be a back-stabber in the business world, but he couldn't use a knife on a woman. He was the type that broke into apartments and took out his rage, frightening a woman that way because he couldn't face the confrontation directly.

At first, Mac hoped it was an act, but it didn't take long to give up on that theory. The man was drunk. The killer wouldn't allow that mistake. The Hunter was cold and ruthlessness. Stewart Hoster was a selfish prig who thought nothing of stealing an underling's work to cover his own inabilities.

It was a waste of time. He wanted to get back to Laken. The desire was past wanting. He needed to get back to her. If Hoster wasn't the killer that meant he was still out there. The knowledge burned in him, and he tried to tamp it down. The only thing keeping him sane was the fact that there was no way he could know where Laken was. She was safe.

"It's all her fault," Hoster whined again. Mac had lost

count of how many times he'd said the same thing, almost word for word.

"They fired me because of what she did – that grandiose show of hers of handing over the blueprints. Saying how he deserved the best and hers were the best. She staged it all to show us up. I'd given her a chance, getting her designs even considered. She should've thanked me. Warner never even would've considered showing her plans. It's all like he said. It's all her fault."

The 'he' caught in Mac's mind, snapping his attention to alert.

"The ungrateful –" the man continued.

"Who said?" Mac cut off Hoster's next tirade.

Laken's former boss jerked, forgetting what he was saying.

"What man?" Mac took two steps toward Hoster, startling him back to soberness. Jonesy also came alert, pulling close.

"The g-guy ... in the b-bar," Hoster stammered out.

"What guy?" Mac demanded, barely holding back his urge to grab the front of his shirt and shake the answer from him. The unease in him shooting to fear.

"I don't know. Just a guy."

"Where'd you meet this guy?

"At the bar across from the place ... the Fun Center. I already told you I followed her there then went into the bar. I was upset. She got me fired. He understood all about backstabbing females. They're all worthless, trying to compete with their betters."

"Did he say that?" Jonesy picked up the questioning.

"Yeah," Hoster looked at him. "He knew what it was like to lose a promotion to a woman who sleeps and steals her way to the top, then walks all over you to get what she wants."

The urged to hit the guy surged again, but Mac tamped it down. "Laken didn't sleep her way to the top, and you're the one who stole from her."

The man still had enough soul to look embarrassed. "She stole the future account, ruined things with Galaxy. It's still her fault."

Mac ignored what he said. "Describe this guy?"

Hoster raised his head, obviously surprised by the request. It took him a second and for Mac to repeat the question before he answered. "A little taller than me, dark hair, but not black. Brown. Late twenties, maybe thirty, I don't know. He was just a guy. I don't look at guys."

"And you didn't ask his name."

Hoster shook his head. "He just got me a couple drinks and talked. He knew what it was like to have a woman walk over you."

Mac could see Hoster slipping back into his moaning again and was done with it. Fear flared to life within him. He needed to get to Laken.

He was out of the room, Jonesy at his side without a word. They'd been partners too long to have to tell the man they were heading to the garage. There was also no need to tell him that, if the man had been at the bar across from the Fun Center, it meant he had either followed them or Hoster there and he could possibly have followed Laken and Connie home.

Mac felt like a fool for not seeing a tail. He fingered Laken's cell phone in his pocket. One of the officers had found it on the floor in the golf room and handed it to him after she'd left.

He pulled out his phone and dialed. "This is Detective MacDaniels, I'd like a unit to do a drive-by for possible intruder at," he gave Jonesy's address as he climbed into the passenger seat. Jonesy had the car headed out of the garage before he disconnected. He made the next call to the captain to fill him in on his thoughts and fears as Jonesy sped through the streets which fortunately were mostly empty at that time of night.

♋

The Hunter moved from shadow to shadow, irritated at the little, yappy dog barking three houses over. If the thing didn't shut up he was going to go slit its throat. He froze when he heard a door open and the owner of the dog yelled out, calling the animal inside. Finally, it was quiet.

He waited several minutes before moving toward the house that held the two women. He didn't care about the one. It was no consequence that she died, but the other had to die so it would all be right. He could feel her now that he was closing in.

Yes. It would finally be right.

Laken fought the covers as she tried to fight the dream from coming. He was hunting. She could feel the exhilaration in him. His excitement ran hot, like the temperature that coursed through her body.

He skirted the house, pulling back in the shadows behind a huge tree trunk when a car came down the street. It pulled into a driveway halfway down the block, and a teenager wearing a fast food uniform got out and ambled into the house.

Kids and dogs should not be seen or heard. The thought hit Laken's mind, and even in the sleeping state, she rejected it. She liked kids and dogs. She wanted to get a dog when she had a place where she could have one. Maybe after she married Mac.

Mac smiled at her coming out of the shadows. He stopped, spun, searching the area, alert, like he had when they left the dumpster, watching everything. He came toward her, striding purposefully then stumbled, his leg going out from under him.

Laken tried to run to him, but her legs were too sluggish to move. She ran harder, faster, but Mac seemed to get farther away. She cried out, but he didn't seem to hear her.

Out of the shadows between them stepped another

figure, the dark raincoat and a hat pulled low, made him a living shadow. She slid to a stop as he came toward her. Laken looked into Hoster's face, then it wasn't his. It fell away into nothingness, a gaping blackness that tore at her soul.

The Hunter turned and looked at Mac, and she knew he was going to keep her from ever reaching him. The Hunter was going to deny her love and life with him.

"No!" she screamed. She would not accept that. She fought harder to run. She had to get to Mac. She wouldn't let The Hunter win.

"You think you can stop me? You think you're better than me?"

The words cut into her mind like a slashing knife. Laken stumbled and fell. Pain ripped at her.

"Women who think they are as good as men don't deserve to live." The Hunter stalked toward her. *"When I kill you, all will be right again."*

"No!" Laken lashed out with her hand. Real pain cut through the dream, but instead of pulling back from it, Laken clung to it, feeling it move up through her arm. She brought her hand to her lips. Her skin felt hot.

She pushed the fever and the throbbing in her head down. "No!" The next scream made it past her lips and Laken jerked awake. Her heart pounded and heat radiated off her. She raised her hand to rub the side of it where it felt like it was bruising.

Laken heard footsteps in the hall and nearly fell out of bed in her haste to get up. The door to her room opened but, instead of the shadowy form of The Hunter, the hall light illuminated Connie, dressed in a short nightgown, much like the one she was wearing.

The woman's eyes darted from the bed to her. "Are you all right?" She sounded breathless, having been abruptly awakened.

Laken let her shoulders slump in relief. "Yes, sorry,

bad d-dream." Laken faltered over the word and knew it wasn't right. *Dream. It was real!* "No. He's here," she gasped, tasting The Hunter's anticipation in the air.

"He's ..., you mean the killer?" Connie visibly relaxed. "It's all right. They've arrested him. They have him at the police station now."

"No!" The word erupted from her with certainty. "Hoster's not The Hunter. He's here."

"Hunter?" Connie looked startled.

"The killer."

"He's here?"

"Yes." The blast of fear hit her almost overwhelming her, but she pushed back.

"Laken," Connie's head was shaking as the woman fought her own internal battle to accept what she was saying. "How could he be here? There's no way he could know where you are?"

"I don't know, maybe he followed us," Laken said over her shoulder searching her clothes for her cell phone. "But he's here. He's close. Where's my cell phone? It was in my pocket when we were golfing."

She threw the hoodie aside and grabbed her pants. The phone wasn't there. "Where's your phone?" She took a step toward Connie and staggered.

"Are you all right?" Connie reached to steady her. "You're burning up."

Laken shook her head to clear it, concentrating a second to push The Hunter back from her mind. For an instant, she could see through him clearly, his hand holding a spade, using it to pry a box from the side of the house. "The phones, he cut the phone line. Your cell phone. We've got to call Mac."

She passed Connie who followed her out of the room, obviously not sure what to think. Probably rethinking her sanity, the thought hit Laken, but she didn't have time to worry about that now. "Where's your cell phone?"

"I ... I think it's in my purse. But there's a phone right here." She lifted the phone from the wall at the end of the hall. "If you want to call Mac ..." her voice died out and she pulled the phone away from her ear and stared down at it like it was a foreign object. "It's dead." She looked at Laken totally stunned.

The air filled with shocked silence only to be shattered by faint scratching at the back of the house. Both women jerked and spun in that direction.

"He's here." This time it was Connie who cried out.

"Do you have a gun?"

Connie was already shaking her head. "I'm not good with guns. Marcus keeps his with him."

"Come on." Laken grabbed her hand pulling her toward the front of the house. "Where's your purse?"

"Closet, by the door."

"Connie, we need to split up," Laken whispered as they moved. "You need to hide. It's me he's after. He won't go for you."

"We need to stick together. We're stronger together." Connie, now in motion, rushed in front of her across the room.

Pulling open the closet door, she grabbed down the large black bag. Instead of sticking her hand in to search, she upended it, dumping out the contents on the floor. The light from the hall glistened off the objects. Connie snatched up the phone and punched nine-one-one.

Laken held her breath waiting for the call to be answered. There was a dull thud at the back door. Laken spun with Connie to look, as she did so, the light coming down the hallway highlighted a three foot long, oddly shaped bag that lean against the back corner of the closet.

Stepping passed Connie, Laken grabbed the bag, pulling it out. With a quick jerk of the zipper, Laken pulled the heavy aluminum baseball bat free just as Connie spoke into the phone. Saying her address then repeating it."

"There's someone trying to break into the house," Connie whispered in the phone. "We think it's the man stabbing women. My husband is Detective Marcus Jones. He's on the case, and I have a witness in the case here with me."

There was a pause. Laken was impressed by how calm Connie was when she continued.

"Yes, that is correct. There are two of us. He's trying to get in the back door."

The words were hardly out of Connie's mouth when Laken heard the grind and splintering of wood as the door was pried open. Without conscious thought, she shoved Connie into the closet.

"Get help, I'll try to delay him." She could see Connie start to object and shook her head. "Please stay here. It's me he's after," she whispered, closing the door quietly.

Her heart pounded as she crossed the room. Pressing her back against the wall by the end of hall, she raised the baseball bat in a batter's stance and listened. Her heart pounded and sweat broke out on her brow.

Her vision blurred as her mind started to slip into the nightmare. She fought it back but not before she caught images of him moving though the kitchen toward the bedroom where she'd been sleeping. The sick wave of his thirst to kill her consumed him. He didn't care that the lights were on in the hall, or Connie was in the house too. He would kill her too because she was there, as though she was of no consequence.

She couldn't let him kill Connie. The thought hit Laken hard. Maybe her facing The Hunter was what was to be. Maybe that was why she had the nightmares, but she was not going to let Connie suffer for it. She tightened her grip on the bat. She was not going down without a fight.

The creak of a floorboard in the hall almost shattered her resolve. A second later the dark cloaked form of The Hunter came into view. Laken swung the bat with all her might, registering at the last second her swing was too low. The man must've caught the motion because he started to pull back, but it wasn't in time to keep the bat from hitting him solidly in his chest.

A grunt escaped him and he staggered back but, liked the possessed man he was, he came right back.

One arm was locked over his chest, and he fought for breath, but it did nothing to lessen the blow of the arm he swung out, catching Laken in the shoulder before she could get the bat back around again. Laken fell back into an end table, tumbling over it onto the couch, knocking the lamp to the floor.

"Think you can take me? Think you're better than I am?" The words ground out like rocks grinding over a surface. He grabbed the leg of the table to shove it out of his way. Laken used the opportunity to roll off the couch to her feet. She staggered a little making her way around the coffee table.

His hat had come off giving her the first look at The Hunter. He wasn't much older than she was. He looked so normal with dark hair, strong cheekbones and a dimple in his chin. She would've thought him good looking if it wasn't for the feverish hatred in his eyes that seemed to consume anything good about him.

Regaining control of her thoughts, she moved back toward the door, drawing him across the room. She had to get him out of the house before he found Connie.

"Stay back." She lifted the bat again, knowing it would infuriate the man as much as deter him.

When he moved closer, she swung out. Unfortunately, this time he was watching and dodged. He attacked before she could bring the bat back around. She screamed and shoved the bat up between them. He grabbed the bat and twisted it free, sending her across the floor, banging back against the front door.

Stunned, she started to sink to the floor until she

locked her knees keeping herself upright. She couldn't let him win.

"It's all your fault!" The Hunter yelled as he walked purposefully toward her, tossing the bat away.

Laken ignored the sound of something breaking as the bat landed in the dining room, fumbling with the lock as the man approached. There was no relief when it clicked unlocked because there was no time to open the door. The Hunter stopped two feet in front of her.

"Your fault." The words spat with venom.

"No," Laken yelled back. "What did I do to you?" she challenged.

"You think you're as good as a man."

She was surprised when he answered, and her mind raced for a way to keep him talking until the police got there. "No, I don't. You're stronger than I am."

He looked shocked then shook his head. "Women are vicious. They sneak up and stab you in the back, using their looks and bodies so you don't see it coming."

Silhouetted in the hallway light, Laken saw the movement of his hand to the pocket of his raincoat and knew from her nightmares he was going for the knife there.

"No," she yelled again and dove for him, dropping her shoulder to ram into his chest where she'd hit him with the bat, the block would've made her brothers proud.

The Hunter was caught by surprise. A sound of pain erupted from his body, echoed by another as he hit the ground. Laken clamped down on her own outcry as her body rebelled from the jarring impact. She longed to lay still but forced herself to roll to the side away from the man.

The hand that caught her wrist locked down so tight she feared it would break her arm. There was no keeping back the cry of pain. He rolled over onto her, his free hand going to her neck, squeezing down.

Laken clawed at the hand as lights flashed in front of

her eyes. She was aware of him pulling her up. The fever slashed through her senses, and she knew he was going for the knife again.

I'm going to die. No! Her mind mutinied against the thought, but there didn't seem to be anything she could do. Then he staggered and staggered again, releasing her. Laken started to sink to the ground only to be caught by Connie.

Laken stumbled several steps back before she realized The Hunter had dropped to the ground. He held his head, but wasn't out. Whatever Connie had hit him with was shattered on the floor around them. By the time Connie got the door open, Laken had enough air back into her lungs to make it outside with Connie on her own power.

The cool night air helped refresh and clear her mind. Though she longed to be met with sirens and police, the night was utterly quiet.

"We have to split up." Laken choked out. Her throat burned from the abuse and sounded unfamiliar.

"We should stay together," Connie objected.

"No," Laken cut her off. "We split up and head to the neighbors on each side."

At that, Connie nodded.

Laken's feet had barely touched the grass when she heard The Hunter crash onto the porch. She forced herself to run and prayed that Connie was doing the same thing in the opposite direction. He couldn't follow them both and she knew it was her he'd go after. She was at the edge of the house when the figure dropped down by her, his dark raincoat bellowing out like a giant set of wings, his hand clawing at her like talons.

She screamed and tumbled to the ground, rolling away, before scrambling back to her feet. The Hunter was angled between her and the next house and the road, so Laken took the only avenue available and headed for the back of the house. The Hunter came after her, only to go back down as he slipped on the damp grass. He was right back up, but the fall had giving her a good ten foot head-start.

Her subconscious yelled she needed to stay close to the house until the police arrived, but panic warred within her to flee. She rounded the corner, her foot coming down on a sprinkler head, gouging it into the skin. Pain almost took her to the ground, but fear kept her going. Moonlight shone off the detached garage and the garbage cans beside it.

The Hunter closed the distance behind her. She fought the urge to look back and pressed for more speed. A hand caught the back of her nightgown, ripping both the material and her feet from under her, dropping her to her knees.

The scream that tried to make it out was cut off in her throat. Again, Laken found herself pulled from the ground and turned to face The Hunter. His arm locked around her, pulling her tight to his chest. She looked up into his eyes and felt the fevered gaze start to overtake her.

Her vision blurred then she saw the vision of her face looking up. Her hair framed her panicked face in wild disarray. Elation filled her. It would finally be right.

"No." She fought back struggling against the hold on her mind and body. The knife was in his hand, she knew. She slammed her head forward, her forehead smashing into his nose, and he staggered back dragging her with him a couple steps, not releasing her.

She wanted to scream again, but before she could, something slammed into them. The blow hit her so hard it knocked the air from her body and sent her flying several feet before smacking to the ground in a pain-fogged stupor.

CʒƏ

Jonesy turned the corner into his subdivision just as the call came over the radio of an intruder and then announced Jonesy's address.

"It's him." Jonesy had already punched the gas before Mac got the words out. His stomach muscles clinched and his hand went to his gun, releasing the strap of the holster.

Jonesy took the next corner skidding and was already accelerating before the car had steadied. He raced up a small hill then fishtailed at the top as he spun them onto the next street. Over the radio, a squad car announced they were four minutes away.

Mac guessed they were less than two minutes if Jonesy kept up their speed, and there was no way he was going to ask him to slow down for caution. He just prayed no one was in their path. Grabbing up the mike, he gave their ETA, gripping the side of the car as they took another turn.

Heavy leaved trees lay down a patchy pattern of moonlight. Mac counted the seconds until they made the last turn onto Jonesy's street. His eyes going immediately to the house near the end of the block, and locked on the two figures.

From the distance, they looked like two fairies frolicking on the lawn. The two split and ran in separate directions. They hadn't gone far when a monstrous black bird seemed to swoop down on one.

Mac knew that was Laken. The pair rolled on the ground then the white clad fairy sprung up dashing toward the back of the house. The shadow, now taking the form of a man, slipped then disappeared after her just before Jonesy brought the car to an abrupt halt at the mouth of his driveway. The headlights caught Connie, freezing her on the spot.

Mac leapt from the car, heading up the driveway to the back yard, letting Marcus catch his wife and see to her safety. He knew Jonesy would be there to back him up as soon as possible.

Mac cursed his leg as it threatened to give out from under him when he stepped down on an uneven section of pavement. He pushed down the pain and forced himself on, praying he could reach Laken in time. He skirted the shrub at the corner of the house, hardly registering the sting when a branch lashed his face.

Laken's short white nightgown was a beacon in the dark. The killer had her clamped to him. Laken was between him and the man, making it impossible to take a shot. Mac wanted to cheer when he saw her slam her head into his nose, but any cheer faltered along with the order to freeze when light glistened over the knife the man raised over her back.

From six feet away, Mac made his leap, his entire concentration on the knife. His hands locked on the arm holding the knife, forcing it up away from Laken as his body plowed into the pair. Mac kept his hold on the arm, his momentum flipping him up over the man.

He felt the bite of metal on his side as he rolled with the killer away from Laken. He ignored the sting of pain and the stronger jab of agony as his leg twist under him as he rolled to get the man farther away from Laken.

The Hunter's knee gouge into his thigh as they finally came to a stop, the killer on top. The Hunter snarled in rage.

Mac tried to push down the searing pain in his leg and concentrate on the man, but his leg was on fire. Pain threatened to blur his vision. It was all he could do to keep his hands locked on the fist that held the knife, which waved dangerously close to his face.

The man was strong, and pressed to the ground limited Mac's movements. He struggled to keep the knife from piercing his chest.

Mac tried to wedge his legs under him to use the leverage to flip them over but his left one gave out, sending up another wave of agony. For a second his mind hazed. It cleared just in time to push the knife back as it dug into his chest.

Pulling on all his will power, Mac shoved up, forcing the man back. He released one hand on the knife arm and sent his fist into the killer's face. From his position on the ground, he couldn't get any back swing to add much power to the punch, but his aim was true, connecting with the nose that Laken had smashed her head into a few minutes earlier.

The killer went over with a cry of agony, blood spurting. Mac struggled up from the ground but had no time to steady himself as the killer dove for him, the knife once more raised, ready to plunge into him.

Mac got an arm up to deflect the blow. Grabbing and twisting to the side, he flipped the man to the ground. The movement put too much pressure on his leg, and it crumpled out from under him.

Mac fought to take in air as shooting pain tried to wipe it out. *Get up!* his mind yelled, but his body was sluggish to answer. He made it to his side and up on one knee, the other refusing to make that motion.

The Hunter, too, was struggling to make it to his feet, and making better progress. The man turned on him again, the knife locked in his outstretched hand. Unable to regain his feet, Mac went for his gun knowing there was little hope of pulling it free before the killer buried the knife into him. Still, it was the only chance.

The killer was only two feet away, and the gun just clearing the holster when Laken's filmy, white clad form tackled The Hunter from the side. The pair tumbled over, landing several feet away but The Hunter didn't stay down.

"Freeze!" Mac yelled, bringing his gun to point.

The killer didn't pause in his movements. "Your fault," he shouted, diving for Laken. The bullet from Mac's gun jerked him back and the one from Jonesy's spun him to the side. The Hunter fell still, his eyes wide in shock as his life flowed out. "No," the word gurgled up, "Can't."

Whatever else he was going to say died on his lips with him. Not that Mac cared to know. He barely got his arm opened to her as Laken dove for him. He fell back not caring about anything but having her locked in his arms. He felt her kisses on his stubbly chin, but she didn't seem to mind that or the sprinkler dampened grass on her exposed skin.

"I love you." She cried the words, and Mac felt his world go right. Nothing mattered, not the dead man a few feet away, the pain in his leg or the knowledge that his time in law enforcement was over. Everything that was important was in his arms.

"Marry me?" He ground the words out.

"Oh, yes." She sealed the promise with a kiss, and Mac realized he'd just asked her to marry him again in the middle of another crime scene, still without a ring. Then again that didn't matter as long as she kept answering "yes".

Epilogue

Three months later.

Laken heard Mac come through the door and turned to greet him with a smile and a slice of strawberry-rhubarb pie. "Well, how was your first day of classes?"

His eyes gleamed, catching sight of her. "Great, but this is better." He took the plate from her, breaking off a piece of pie, but instead of taking the bite, he waved it in front of her face. "Open up."

She laughed and complied, not at all surprised when his lips followed the bite to her mouth. After three weeks of marriage, Laken was getting used to Mac's idea of sharing. As the kiss continued, Laken felt her heart jump and a wave of heat enveloped her. The only fevers she had now were raised by Mac.

She figured life couldn't get much better. Mac had gotten the job at the university. Mr. Sherman had accepted the initial plans for his new building. They had found the perfect house with a nice, large yard. They had an incredible honeymoon filled with sun and each other. And after a week of moving in, the boxes were gone and they were settled into their new home.

Her dreams were coming true and they were all wonderful, full of life and love.

About the Author

I grew up in a small town in Wyoming loving the outdoors, sports, art, and reading Hardy Boys books. After reading them all at least a half dozen times, I started writing my own stories.

Thirty years ago I married a wonderful, honorable man. I have five children and eleven grandchildren. I love traveling. Through my husband's work and vacations, I have visited much of the United States, all over Western Europe, Canada, Mexico, China, Thailand, Cambodia and Australia, giving me many intriguing locations and experiences for my stories.

I am a storyteller. I write the classic hero story because I think there's a need for more heroes, love, and adventure in our lives. I'm not out to change the world with my writing; I'm just hoping to make your day a little better.

Hope you enjoy.
Alysia S. Knight

Please feel free to visit me through my website:

www.alysiasknight.com